THE ORISIS CODE

MARCUS FLINT

THE ORISIS CODE

This book is a work of fiction. The characters, incidents, and dialogs are products of the author's imagination and are not to be construed

as accurate. Any resemblance to actual events or persons, living or dead, is coincidental.

Contents

Prologue

In ancient Egypt, where the sands whisper tales of pharaohs and gods, Osiris's name resonates through the ages as a symbol of power, rebirth, and eternal life. Osiris, the god of the afterlife and the underworld, was revered as a benevolent ruler and judge of the dead, embodying the cycle of life, death, and resurrection in Egyptian mythology.

The enigmatic *Osiris Code* was discovered within this rich tapestry of ancient lore, hidden within the intricate hieroglyphics of a forgotten tomb. The code, a cryptic puzzle of symbols and secrets, held the key to unlocking untold riches and ancient knowledge, drawing the attention of scholars, treasure hunters, and those willing to kill to possess its power.

Dr. Jonathan Hartley, a brilliant historian with a passion for uncovering the mysteries of the past, stumbled upon the *Osiris Code* during his research in Egypt. As he delved deeper into the code's secrets, he revealed a connection to the myth of Osiris, realizing that the code held the promise of unlocking the secrets of life and death, power, and rebirth.

Unbeknownst to Dr. Hartley, the discovery of the *Osiris Code* set off a dangerous treasure hunt that would blur the lines between past and present, myth and reality. As he embarked on a perilous journey to decipher the code's true significance, he was entangled in a web of deception, risky pursuits, and unexpected alliances, where the fate of ancient treasures and modern lives hung in the balance. The *Osiris Code* held the power to change everything, and Dr. Hartley's quest to unlock its mysteries would lead him down the path of danger, discovery, and destiny.

Chapter 1

The trowel scraped softly against the crumbling mortar as Evan carefully brushed away the centuries of accumulated dirt. Ancient hieroglyphics slowly emerged on the wall before him, their carved images coming into focus for the first time in millennia.

Evan's pulse quickened as he revealed more of the intricate carvings. He lived for this - the thrill of discovery, of being the first to gaze upon these symbols in over two thousand years. As an Egyptologist, Evan found nothing more exciting than unearthing the mysteries of this ancient civilization.

"Incredible," he murmured, examining the symbols more closely. He recognized depictions of Egyptian gods and pharaohs, but there were unfamiliar elements too. What secrets might they reveal? Evan's mind raced with possibilities even as he meticulously documented every detail.

Glancing at his watch, Evan hesitated. He was tempted to keep working as more questions arose, but he knew the importance of a systematic approach. With a sigh, he began carefully packing his tools. The codex would still be here tomorrow, but he had taken the first step in unraveling its secrets. The familiar fire of curiosity burned within Evan as he cast one last longing look at the hieroglyphs. He would return, and one day, he would decode the messages they held. But for now, patience. The past was not going anywhere.

Evan returned to the dig site at dawn, eager to examine the hieroglyphs further.

As the rising sun illuminated the ancient carvings, he leaned in with his magnifying glass and scrutinized every detail.

One section in particular drew his attention - a series of bird symbols repeating at regular intervals. Evan quickly cross-referenced his reference books.

"The god Horus," he murmured. This was unusual - Horus was typically depicted as a falcon, not a simple bird. What was the significance?

Evan traced the sequence of Horus symbols with his finger. There seemed to be a pattern, but it wasn't easy to discern at first glance. He carefully copied the symbols into his notebook, numbering each occurrence.

After finishing the transcription, Evan stared at the page intently. Suddenly, he saw it - every seventh Horus was slightly altered, its wings outstretched.

"A code," Evan whispered, his pulse quickening. This had to mark divisions in the text, like spaces between words. He was no longer gazing at an artistic frieze but a message.

Glancing anxiously, Evan rolled up his notes and slipped them into his bag. He would decipher this code, but he needed to take precautions. Who knew what ancient secrets these hieroglyphs might reveal?

Evan's mind raced as he headed back to his tent. He was on the cusp of a significant discovery—he could feel it. All his years of study he had led to this moment. With meticulous care and just the right amount of cunning, he would unravel the mysteries of the past.

Evan hurried back to his tent, his mind spinning with questions. What secrets did these ancient symbols contain? And who else might be seeking to uncover them?

He knew he couldn't decipher the code at the dig site. It was too exposed and vulnerable. He needed to get somewhere secure to study the symbols in depth.

Furtively glancing, Evan pulled out his notes and began transcribing the hieroglyphs into his encrypted digital journal. He would leave no trail for potential enemies to follow, so he erased the original pages and packed his bag.

The night was falling as Evan slipped out of his tent and made his way stealthily through the sleeping archaeological camp. Reaching his dusty old Land Rover, he quickly loaded his gear and started the engine. As the vehicle rumbled into the darkness, Evan felt his pulse quicken. He was on the hunt for answers now and wouldn't stop until he had uncovered the whole meaning of the ancient code.

The road was rough and the night deep, but Evan drove on relentlessly. His mind turned over the discovered symbols, seeking patterns and connections. This code had been hidden for millennia - now, finally, it would give up its secrets.

Evan knew he was tampering with powerful forces, but his insatiable curiosity drove him forward. All his training and expertise had prepared him for this moment. Come what may, he would decipher this message and reveal the knowledge hidden within. The mysteries of the past were calling to him across the centuries—and he would answer.

Evan drove through the night, fueled by determination and curiosity. As the first rays of dawn crept over the horizon, he finally reached his safehouse - an isolated cabin far from prying eyes.

He wasted no time, hurried inside, and unpacked his notes and research materials. Spreading everything on the table, Evan got to work analyzing the symbols and hieroglyphs he had uncovered.

Hours passed in focused silence as he pored over the ancient code, searching for patterns and meaning. His eyes grew heavy with fatigue, but Evan persisted, driven by an almost obsessive need to decipher this secret message.

By late afternoon, frustration began setting in. The code was complex, and Evan was going in circles, unable to make sense of certain symbols and repetitive sequences. He paced the cabin, racking his brain, the hieroglyphs blurring together in his exhausted mind.

"There must be some logic to this," he muttered, running his hand through his messy hair. Evan knew giving up was not an option when he was so close. The answer was here; he had to clear his mind and approach it from a new angle.

Splashing cold water on his face, Evan took a deep breath. He forced himself to relax and return to the code with fresh eyes. There had to be a breakthrough soon. The secrets of the ancient world were within his grasp - and he would not let them slip away.

Sitting back at the table, Evan carefully reviewed each symbol and glyph again. A few oddities jumped out as he studied them, opening his mind to new possibilities.

"There's a pattern here after all," he realized with growing excitement. Three particular hieroglyphs repeated at oddly regular intervals. When viewed together, they seemed to form a sequence.

His pulse quickened, and Evan grabbed a blank sheet and began writing the symbols down in the order of their repetition. A message was emerging, but it was still fragmented. He had uncovered only a portion of the code.

Still, the few ancient Egyptian words now visible on the page were enough to make his hair stand on end:

"Hidden...beneath...sacred temple...key...afterlife..."

"My god," Evan whispered, sitting back in his chair. His hands trembled slightly as the significance sank in. This code pointed to something buried near an ancient temple - something of immense value and purpose. He was on the verge of a momentous discovery.

But Evan knew the journey had only just begun. Danger lurked ahead; he could feel it. For now, he allowed himself a moment to breathe and reflect. Then, with renewed vigor, he turned back to the symbols. He had to crack the rest of this code before others uncovered its secret. The race was on.

The following day, Evan arrived at the dig site before sunrise, eager to get back to work deciphering the code. As the first rays of light crept over the ancient ruins, he carefully set up his tools and notebooks, laying everything out.

With a deep breath, Evan again focused on the hieroglyphs. "All right, my friends," he murmured, "let's see what other secrets you hold."

He started where he had left off, meticulously analyzing each symbol and cross-referencing his notes. Slowly but surely, the code was unraveling before him.

After several hours of intense concentration, Evan sat back, removed his glasses, and rubbed his eyes. He had filled several more pages with translations, but there still needed to be more.

"Almost there," he told himself. "Just a little more."

He knew he was tantalizingly close to deciphering the entire message. But this last part was proving stubbornly elusive, with cryptic references to trials along the path and hidden keys.

Evan was no stranger to challenges, however. He had devoted his life to unraveling ancient mysteries just like this. With a wry smile, he leaned forward again with renewed determination.

"Alright, let's finish this," he declared to the empty ruins. He was sure the code would give up its secrets today. All he needed was perseverance, intuition, and a little luck.

Chapter 2

Evan hunched over his desk, surrounded by stacks of ancient Egyptian texts and artifacts. His glasses perched precariously on the edge of his nose as he pored over a cryptic message scrawled across a crumbling papyrus scroll. He scribbled furiously, making connections between symbols, his mind racing.

He had stayed in this office for two days, neglecting sleep and meals in his obsession. Red Bull cans and empty takeout containers littered the area around him. His stubble had grown into an unkempt beard, and his clothes were messy. But his eyes remained sharp and focused behind his glasses. All that existed now was this code and its secrets about a long-lost Egyptian treasure.

Evan's pulse quickened as he worked through a sequence of hieroglyphs. This code was complex, but he was making progress. A breakthrough was close; he could feel it. The answers were here in these ancient texts if he could just put the pieces together.

His eyes narrowed, gleaming with determination. He would not rest until he cracked this puzzle. The mysteries of the past called to him, and he would answer, no matter the cost.

Three sharp knocks at the door jolted Evan from his intense concentration. He glanced up, startled, as the door creaked open.

"Hey Evan, got a minute?"

Dr. Sarah Johnson poked her head in, her long black hair falling across her face. Evan straightened up and attempted to smooth down his disheveled clothes.

"Sarah! Come on in," he said, shuffling aside some of the clutter on his desk.

Sarah stepped inside, surveying the chaotic scene with amusement dancing in her eyes.

"Working hard, I see," she said wryly.

Evan gave her a sheepish grin. "You know me, once I sink my teeth into a puzzle, I can't let go."

His expression turned serious again. "But this time, I think I'm onto something big."

He grabbed the papyrus scroll, tracing his finger along the cryptic symbols etched into the ancient parchment.

"This code could lead us to the lost tomb of Pharaoh Seti. Buried treasure beyond imagination." Excitement crept into his voice.

As she studied the scroll, Sarah leaned in, curiosity sparking in her gaze. Evan launched into an explanation, pointing out key hieroglyphs and his interpretations. Her brows knit together in concentration as she listened.

"This changes everything we thought we knew about Seti's reign," she said. "Are you sure about this?"

Evan nodded firmly. "I need to decipher the last section fully, but I know the answers are here. Whatever secrets are hidden in that tomb, we're going to be the ones to uncover them."

Sarah met his determined gaze with her look of resolve. "Then let's get to work," she said.

Sarah's eyes narrowed as she scrutinized the hieroglyphs, her mind racing to decode the intricate symbols.

"This glyph here, the one that looks like an ostrich feather. Have you considered it could represent the god Amun?" she asked.

Evan paused, leaning in to examine the marking more closely. "I thought it was just denoting status or royalty, but you might be onto something."

He grabbed a large leatherbound book and flipped through the pages. "Amun was often depicted with an ostrich feather, and he was the patron god of Pharaoh Seti."

Sarah nodded, pleased that her hunch was panning out. "Exactly. So following that thinking puts a whole new spin on the rest of the message."

The two scholars launched into an animated debate, bouncing theories and interpretations back and forth. Evan's initial excitement was replaced by frustration as they hit dead ends. Sarah remained coolly analytical, turning over clues in her mind.

"Here," she said finally, tapping a section of text. "I think this is referring to the temple of Amun in Karnak. Perhaps the tomb is hidden somewhere nearby."

Evan's eyes lit up. "Brilliant! I can't believe I missed that connection."

He grinned at Sarah. "Have I mentioned you're a genius?"

She laughed. "Flattery will get you everywhere." Her expression grew serious again. "If we're right about this, we're one step closer to uncovering a find of a lifetime."

Evan met her gaze with a knowing look. The thrill of discovery still lay ahead of them, but they were on the path to unraveling the scroll's secrets. The game was afoot.

Evan's excitement dimmed as he scrutinized the next section of hieroglyphs. The symbols were familiar yet arranged in confusing patterns he couldn't decipher. He scribbled notes feverishly, trying to unlock the meaning.

They passed hours without a breakthrough. Evan's shoulders slumped as he tossed his pen down in frustration. This code was proving to be maddeningly complex.

He stood and paced the room, raking his hands through his hair. Some key that would make the jumble of signs intelligible had to be missing. Evan was not easily deterred, especially with the tantalizing prospect of a lost tomb so close.

Sarah watched him, seeing the toll this puzzle was taking. She rose and joined him at the table.

"Let's try looking at it another way," she suggested gently. Drawing on her knowledge of Egyptian mythology, she traced connections between symbols and gods, teasing out subtleties.

Evan listened intently as Sarah shed new light on the code's intricacies. Her insights unlocked fresh pathways in his mind, and possibilities took shape where there had only been confusion.

"You're brilliant, Sarah!" Evan exclaimed, a renewed energy in his voice. "I think you've cracked it."

The two smiled, the electric thrill of discovery passing between them. The answers were close now, tantalizingly within their grasp. The secrets of the code would soon be theirs.

Sarah leaned over the table, eyes bright with excitement as she examined the symbols. "Look here, the repeated motif of the scarab beetle. I think it's a clue to location."

Evan nodded, following her train of thought. "Scarab tombs were typically built near the Valley of the Kings."

They poured over maps and texts, searching for correlations. Piece by piece, the message revealed itself to their probing minds.

"There!" Evan jabbed his finger at an obscure marking. "The cliffs near Deir el-Bahari. That must be it."

Sarah met his eyes, seeing the same fiery glow. "We've found it," she breathed. After weeks of frustration, persistence and teamwork had revealed the answer.

Evan squeezed her shoulder, smiling. "We make a good team." The spark between them was unmistakable. United by curiosity and discovery, they stood on the cusp of revelation.

The secret tomb awaited, hidden for millennia yet patient. Soon, it would yield its treasures to those clever enough to decipher its coded invitation. Evan and Sarah had proven worthy of its secrets. The adventure was beginning.

Sarah's eyes shone with determination as she traced her finger along the map. "The Valley of the Kings. That's where we need to go next."

Evan nodded, feeling a swell of anticipation. "We'll have to move quickly. This discovery won't stay secret once others connect the same clues."

Sarah's lips pressed into a thin line. Those who would plunder such sites for profit and glory often threatened their intellectual pursuit. She and Evan shared a passion for knowledge and protecting the integrity of their discoveries.

"If we start packing now, we can be on a flight to Cairo tomorrow," Evan said, gathering his notes. "I know some local guides who can take us to the site."

Sarah grinned, her initial wariness replaced by thrilled excitement. "Let's do it. This is the kind of a lifetime."

Evan smiled back. With Sarah by his side, he felt he could unravel even the most obscure secrets of history. Her intellect and courage perfectly complemented his own.

As they prepared for the next leg of their journey, Evan knew he had found more than one colleague in Sarah. They now stood poised on the edge of revelation, ready to blaze together. The true treasure was not gold or jewels but the bond formed through this adventure. The future shone brightly for them both.

Chapter 3

The night air was still, almost suffocating in its silence. Evan crept along the museum's exterior wall, his footsteps muffled against the cobblestones. Up ahead, a black van idled at the loading dock, its headlights off. Evan's pulse quickened. They were already here.

With practiced efficiency, four figures emerged from the van dressed entirely in black, faces obscured by ski masks. Evan pressed himself into the shadows, watching as they approached the service entrance. One man produced a device from his pack and held it to the keypad. A few seconds later, a faint click sounded, and the door swung open.

"Let's move," said a low voice. The man who had opened the door slipped inside, the others filing in behind him.

Evan inched forward, keeping to the darkness. He reached the door just before it closed and caught it with his fingertips. Taking a deep breath, he followed them inside.

The intruders easily navigated the halls, making their way toward the new exhibit of Egyptian antiquities. Ancient statues lined the room, bathed in the moonlight streaming through the skylights. The men spread out and began packing the more minor artifacts into padded crates.

Their leader headed straight for the centerpiece - a priceless sarcophagus adorned with gold and jewels. Evan's jaw clenched. He knew what was inside, even if the public didn't: clues to finding the wealthiest tomb in history lost for millennia.

Evan stepped from the shadows as the man prepared to open the coffin. "I wouldn't do that if I were you."

The leader turned, his eyes narrowing. "Dr. Reynolds. I might find you here." Anton Voronov's sharp accent cut through the silence.

Evan met his icy stare. "I can't let you take that."

Anton's mouth curved into a cruel smile. "Unfortunately, you have no choice." He raised a silenced pistol and fired.

Evan dove behind a statue as the shot rang out, the bullet pinging off the marble. He scrambled into a crouch, peering around the base of the monument.

Anton strode toward the coffin, beckoning his men over. "Ignore the doctor. Focus on the task at hand."

As the henchmen surrounded their leader, one figure hung back, lingering in the shadows. She moved with feline grace, her footsteps silent on the tile floor. When she stepped into a shaft of moonlight, her features were momentarily illuminated - high cheekbones, piercing eyes, and a long braid of chestnut hair.

Nadia Zamani. Evan had heard rumors of Anton's most trusted assassin but had never seen her in the flesh. As she watched the men work, her focus was unwavering, one hand resting lightly on the hilt of a dagger on her hip. Evan did not doubt that she could draw the blade and slit a throat in the blink of an eye.

He needed to stop them, but he was outnumbered and outgunned. Evan's mind raced, analyzing the room for anything he could use to his advantage. A noise at the end of the hall made him turn. Sarah stood there, a fire extinguisher in hand. She raised her eyebrows at Evan, glancing meaningfully at the extinguisher.

A distraction. Perfect. Evan gave her a slight nod.

The fire extinguisher sailed through the air on Sarah's signal, clattering to the floor near Anton's feet. The men shouted in surprise, blinded by the plume of white smoke. In the chaos, Evan and Sarah rushed in, hoping to reach the coffin first. The treasure hunters were disoriented, but not for long. Nadia recovered quickly, drawing her blade as she moved to intercept the two archaeologists.

This was about to get ugly.

Sarah acted instinctually, grabbing a nearby vase and smashing it over Nadia's head. The assassin stumbled, momentarily stunned.

"Go!" Sarah shouted to Evan. "I'll hold her off!"

Evan raced for the casket. Anton's men shouted curses, fumbling to grab their weapons. But Evan was faster. He threw open the heavy stone lid, frantically scanning the contents. There, tucked against the mummified body, was a small gold statue of Anubis. Evan grabbed it, feeling a surge of triumph.

This is what Anton was after—the key to finding the lost tomb.

Behind him, Sarah cried out. Evan whirled to see Nadia pressing a knife to Sarah's throat. Anton strode forward, murder in his eyes.

"Give it to me," he growled.

Evan hesitated. He couldn't let Anton get the statue, but Sarah...

Anton snapped his fingers. One of his men cocked a gun, aiming at Evan.

"Now!" Anton barked.

With no choice, Evan held out the golden statue. Anton snatched it gleefully.

"You've served your purpose," he sneered. "Kill them."

Evan braced himself as the man aimed his gun. But an explosion rocked the building. Dust rained down as part of the ceiling collapsed, blocking Anton's escape route. Through the hole peered a familiar face.

"Need some help?" Jake asked with a grin.

In the confusion, Sarah broke free of Nadia's grip. The treasure hunters scrambled for cover as Jake lobbed a flash grenade. Evan grabbed Sarah's hand and followed Jake out through the crumbling wall. They had lost the statue, but they still had their lives.

And Evan had gotten a good, long look at that statue. Its mysteries were not lost yet. The race for Egypt's most significant treasure was still ongoing.

Sarah coughed as dust swirled around them. The blast had allowed them to escape Anton and his goons, but they weren't out of danger yet.

"This way!" Jake shouted, leading them down a narrow alley. Evan glanced back, half expecting to see Anton's men bursting out of the rubble in pursuit.

Sarah winced, clutching her arm where Nadia's knife had cut her. "We have to keep moving," she said through gritted teeth. "Anton won't give up that easily."

Evan put his arm around her waist, supporting her as they hurried after Jake. His mind raced, trying to process what he'd learned from the statue before Anton snatched it away. Symbols and constellations point to something hidden in the night sky over Giza. It was a clue, but to what?

He replayed the details in his mind's eye. Evan had always had a knack for memorizing things, and that skill made him one of the world's leading Egyptologists.

"Did you get a good look at it?" Sarah asked, reading his thoughts.

"Enough," Evan said. "We'll figure it out, don't worry-"

He was cut off by the screech of tires ahead. A black SUV skidded around the corner, nearly hitting them as they darted out of its path. Evan's heart sank. Anton had found them already.

This wasn't over yet. Not by a long shot.

Sarah's breath caught as the SUV's tinted window rolled down. She tensed, ready to fight or run. But it wasn't Anton's men.

"Mom?!" Jake exclaimed in disbelief.

Sarah blinked, equally shocked to see Jake's mother behind the wheel. She hadn't seen her since...

"Get in, quickly!" Jake's mom shouted. Sarah didn't hesitate, bundling into the backseat with Evan. Jake jumped in next to his mother and bombarded her with questions.

"What are you doing here? How did you find us?"

"There's no time to explain," she said, flooring the gas pedal.

"I got a message saying you were all in danger."

Evan and Sarah exchanged a grim look. Anton's reach was further than they realized if he could get to Jake's family.

"We need to get off the grid," Evan said. "Somewhere, Anton won't think to look."

Jake's mom nodded. "I know a place. An old family cabin, hours from here."

It wasn't ideal, but it was better than nothing. They needed time to unravel the clues Evan had gleaned without Anton's men breathing down their necks.

Sarah winced again as they hit a bump in the road, jostling her injured arm. Jake's mom glanced back, concern creasing her brow.

"The First aid kit is under the seat. Let's patch you up and get out of here."

Sarah nodded, adrenaline still pumping through her veins. They were in deep now, but the answers were within their grasp. She had to believe this setback was only temporary. The treasure - and the truth - were close. They just had to stay alive long enough to find them.

Sarah rifled through the first aid kit with her good arm, searching for something to dress her wound. The gash on her bicep from the knife fight was still oozing blood, but she'd have to make do with what they had in the car.

As Jake's mom raced down the winding mountain roads, Evan watched out the back window. So far, there had been no sign of their pursuers, but Evan knew Anton's men wouldn't give up so easily.

"We need to switch vehicles as soon as possible," Evan said. "They've probably got a tracker on this one."

Jake's mom nodded, her lips pressed in a thin line. She was taking this remarkably well for someone who just had their life upended. But protecting her son was her top priority.

Speaking of which, Jake was still asking rapid-fire questions in the back seat. "So, these guys are after the treasure, too? The one from Dad's old case?"

"Yes," his mom replied tersely. "We need to lay low until your father can handle this."

Jake looked like he wanted to protest but held his tongue. Evan felt for the kid. He knew what it was like to have everything you thought you knew about your family questioned.

Sarah finished bandaging her arm and leaned back with a pained sigh. "We need to decrypt the riddle your dad left. It's the only way to stay ahead of Anton."

Evan nodded. "Once we have the treasure's location, we can use it as leverage. Anton will have to negotiate if he wants it."

It was a long shot, but they're only playing right now. Evan hoped they could crack the code before Anton's men caught up to them again. The subsequent encounter might not end in their favor.

Chapter 4

The flickering lamplight cast an amber glow across the cluttered room, glinting off the artifacts and relics strewn across every surface. Evan leaned back in his creaking leather chair, his keen eyes alight behind his glasses as he studied the ancient papyrus scroll on the desk before him.

"This code could change everything we thought we knew about the 18th dynasty," he said, his voice taut with excitement. Across from him, Sarah nodded, her dark eyes intense.

"If it's authentic," she cautioned, though her curiosity was piqued. She reached for a heavy, leather-bound tome, its pages cracked and yellowed. Flipping it open, her slender fingers traced the faded hieroglyphics inked across the brittle papyrus pages.

"Look here," she murmured, sliding the book toward Evan and tapping a series of symbols. "This passage refers to the 'Hidden One,' which could be a reference to"

"Akhenaten," Evan finished, his pulse quickening as the implications dawned on him. He scrutinized the symbols, mentally decoding the ancient text. This was the breakthrough they had been searching for, a key to unraveling secrets lost to the sands of time.

Sarah watched him closely, noting the determined set of his jaw. She knew that look well—the thirst for answers that drove him relentlessly onward. She understood this passion, yet it still gave her pause. Some secrets were meant to remain buried.

Sarah leaned back in her chair, regarding Evan thoughtfully. "If this code does relate to Akhenaten, it could completely rewrite history," she mused. "But where do we go from here?"

Evan's eyes gleamed behind his glasses as he traced a symbol on the scroll - a falcon with outstretched wings. "The Tomb of Horus," he murmured. "I read about a theory that Akhenaten may have been buried there secretly, against the wishes of the priests who tried to erase him from history."

Sarah nodded slowly, intrigued. The Tomb of Horus, located deep within the Valley of the Kings, was one of the most enigmatic sites in Egypt. Rumors swirled of hidden chambers and deadly curses, all to protect the secrets interred within.

"It's dangerous," she cautioned. "We'd be going in blind."

"That's why we need to prepare," Evan said firmly. "We'll study all the relevant texts and maps first and bring only essential gear that won't weigh us down. It's a calculated risk." His eyes lit up, alight with the lure of revelation.

Sarah hesitated, then nodded. The thrill of discovery had hooked her, too. They worked late into the night, preparing for the journey ahead. The dust of centuries past swirled around them as they pursued ancient secrets, long hidden but never forgotten.

The wind howled through the narrow valley, scattering sand and debris. Evan and Sarah stood at the entrance of the Tomb of Horus, peering into the gaping darkness before them.

Sarah clicked on her flashlight, casting a circle of light onto the carved hieroglyphs lining the walls. Tracing her fingers over the symbols, her brow furrowed in concentration, she looked around.

"These look like the same markings from the scroll," she murmured. "We must be on the right track."

Evan nodded, examining a depiction of the falcon-headed god. "Horus was said to have protected the pharaohs. Let's hope he still guards this place."

With cautious steps, they ventured inside. The air was heavy with the scent of ancient incense and powdered earth, and their flashlight beams darted around nervously.

Sarah gasped as a giant beetle scuttled across their path. Evan put a reassuring hand on her shoulder.

"It's just us and the bugs down here," he said softly.

They arrived at a chamber with a high, arched ceiling. Sarah quickly set up a tripod and camera to document the writing on the walls, and Evan's flashlight illuminated a series of symbols.

"These look nearly identical to the code," he muttered excitedly. "This must be key to deciphering it."

Sarah nodded, snapping photos from every angle. "We'll analyze these back at the lab. I have a good feeling about this place."

Evan smiled at her. "Then let's keep searching. I sense we're close to something big."

Their footsteps echoed through the silent depths as they ventured farther into the ancient tomb, drawn by mystery and promise of revelation. The past was starting to unveil its secrets.

They moved deeper into the tomb, their flashlights cutting through the inky darkness. The air grew heavier and more stagnant as they descended crumbling staircases.

Suddenly, Sarah stopped short. "Do you hear that?" she whispered.

Evan strained his ears. A soft, rhythmic clicking echoed up ahead.

"Could just be the structure settling," Evan offered, but his furrowed brow betrayed his uncertainty.

They proceeded with caution, testing each step before putting their weight down. The clicking grew louder.

As she rounded a corner, Sarah stifled a scream. A giant scorpion scuttled across the passage and disappeared into a crevice.

"It's alright, just keep moving," Evan urged.

The passage narrowed, forcing them to turn sideways to squeeze through. Sarah's shirt snagged on a jagged rock, tearing the fabric.

"This tomb wasn't meant for the living," she grumbled.

Finally, the passage opened into a large burial chamber. Intricate murals, brilliantly colored despite the millennia, covered the walls.

"Incredible," breathed Evan. "These depict the battle between Horus and Set. Look - hieroglyphics!"

Sarah hurriedly set up her equipment. She photographed the murals from multiple angles while Evan rubbed the text.

"This is the motherlode," Evan said excitedly. "With this, we can finally crack the code."

Sarah nodded triumphantly. "Let's get this back to the lab. I have a feeling we're getting close to something big."

Their voices echoed off the ancient stones as they prepared to depart, hoping the next clue would soon be within their grasp.

Sarah carefully rolled the rubbings and tucked them into her pack while Evan gave the chamber one final sweep. He felt slight indentation as he ran his hand along the back wall. Pushing on it caused a hidden panel to slide open.

"Sarah, look at this!" Evan called out.

Inside the small, dark space sat a glint of gold. Sarah shone her flashlight on the object - a small golden amulet shaped like a falcon.

"It's the amulet of Horus," she whispered reverently. She reached in and lifted it gently. The fine details of the wings and head were exquisitely crafted.

"This must be the key to the next step of the code," Evan said.

Sarah nodded. "Let's keep moving. If this amulet were hidden here, more clues would be ahead."

With renewed vigor, they ventured deeper into the tomb. The air grew heavier, and they had to duck under cobwebs and step over debris piles.

Then Evan paused, holding up his hand. "Do you hear that?" A faint rumbling echoed from up ahead.

"The structure could be weak here," Sarah said nervously.

They inched forward until the passage opened into a large burial vault. Evan swept his light over the walls. "More murals, more text. This is exactly what we're looking for."

But as he stepped forward, Sarah grabbed his shoulder. "Wait!"

A tile sank under his weight. Suddenly, the rumbling intensified. Large rocks broke free from the ceiling. Sarah yanked Evan back as the stones smashed down, blocking the passage behind them.

"That was close," Evan panted. "We'll have to find another way out."

Sarah gripped the amulet tightly. "Let's keep going. The answers we're looking for must be near."

Sarah and Evan stepped carefully into the burial vault, sweeping their flashlights over the intricate hieroglyphs and paintings adorning the walls. Sarah's eyes widened as she made out scenes depicting gods, pharaohs, and mythical beasts.

"This must be the chamber dedicated to Horus," she murmured. "Look - there are passages from The Book of the Dead."

Evan traced his fingers over the deeply carved symbols. "These look just like the code fragments we found. It's no coincidence."

He stepped back, surveying the room. At the far end stood an imposing stone statue of Horus, his wings outstretched.

"There must be a hidden message here, guiding us to the next step," Evan said. He began examining the walls methodically while Sarah studied the statue's base.

After several minutes, Sarah called out, "Evan, look at this." She pointed to a series of symbols at the statue's feet. Evan knelt beside her.

"It's a sequence of hieroglyphs and numbers," he said excitedly. "This perfectly aligns with the partial code we decrypted back home."

Together, they transcribed the entire sequence into their notebooks. Triumph surged through them as they worked, and the final secrets were within their grasp.

"If we combine this with the amulet, I think we can pinpoint the treasure's location," Evan said. "We're so close now. I can feel it."

Sarah grinned. "Let's get everything we need documented. Then we can start heading for the inner burial chamber."

With renewed vigor, they set to work capturing every detail. The answers they sought were now within reach, waiting to be uncovered.

Sarah carefully photographed each symbol while Evan took rubbings. As they worked, anticipation built inside them. The inner burial chamber and its secrets awaited.

Evan and Sarah gathered their gear after thoroughly documenting the statue and hieroglyphs. Sarah pulled out a detailed map of the tomb and traced their route.

"The chamber should be through that passageway," she said, pointing to a dark, narrow opening across from the statue. Evan shone his flashlight down the passage. It was ominously silent.

"Let's do this," he said, a determined glint in his eyes. Side by side, they entered the passageway. Sarah felt her pulse quicken. Her senses were on high alert, ready to detect hidden traps.

The passage twisted and turned, sloping gradually downward. Their flashlight beams danced across the walls, illuminating carved images of gods and pharaohs.

"It's like we're descending into the underworld itself," Sarah murmured.

After several tense minutes, the passage opened into a large chamber. Evan and Sarah stepped forward reverently. This was it—the inner sanctum. Their eyes adjusted to the darkness, taking in the sight before them.

A giant sealed stone door marked with falcon motifs stood at the room's far end. Sarah's breath caught in her throat. Beyond it lay the treasure and revelation they had risked everything to find.

"This is it," Evan whispered. "The moment of truth." Gripped by excitement, they approached the door. The culmination of their efforts was at hand. With pounding hearts, they prepared to unlock its secrets.

Chapter 5

Evan hunched over the ancient scroll, magnifying glass in hand. Hieroglyphs swam before his eyes, their secrets still locked away.

"This symbol here," he murmured. "It must represent the winding Nile. See how it curves?"

Sarah nodded, leaning in close. Her hair brushed Evan's shoulder, and he caught a whiff of jasmine. He tried to focus on the scroll, but his mind wandered to their earlier embrace.

The scrape of stone on stone jolted him back. Sarah jerked her head up, her eyes narrowing. She glanced at the window, where a shadowy figure lurked.

Evan's heart quickened. Carefully, he rolled the scroll and slipped it into his bag. He felt Sarah's tension mirrored in himself. Who was this stranger? Friend or foe?

Sarah moved soundlessly to the door and peered out. The figure was advancing steadily through the gloom. She turned back, face taut.

"We should go," she mouthed.

Evan agreed. This site was remote and isolated. If the stranger meant harm...

He swept the remaining scrolls into his pack. Sarah produced a flashlight from her pocket and clicked it on, illuminating a rear exit.

Staying low, they slipped out the back way. They were pressed close the night as they hurried across the sandy ground. Evan strained his ears but heard only the whisper of wind.

At last, they reached the jeep's shelter. Evan started the engine, the roar shattering the silence. As they peeled away, he met Sarah's eyes. Though neither spoke, they shared the same thought.

This was just the beginning. The danger was coming.

The jeep's headlights cut through the darkness as Evan drove down the winding desert road. He glanced at Sarah in the passenger seat, her jaw clenched and her gaze fixed ahead.

"Who do you think that was back there?" Evan finally said.

Sarah shook her head. "I don't know, but they were watching us. This dig is supposed to be secret."

Evan gripped the wheel tighter, possibilities racing through his mind. "Could it be Preston? Or someone from the university?"

"Maybe," Sarah said. "Or it could be something more sinister."

Evan frowned. He knew Sarah's past made her quick to suspect foul play. But what nefarious purpose could someone have for following them here?

His thoughts were interrupted by a vehicle approaching fast behind them. Evan checked the mirror. A black SUV barreled down on their bumper.

"We've got company," he said briefly.

Sarah turned to look. "Can you lose them?"

"I'll try." Evan pressed the gas pedal down, picking up speed on the desert road. The SUV kept pace effortlessly. Evan took a hard right and left, trying to shake their tail, but the SUV stayed glued behind them.

Up ahead, Evan spied a small side road half-hidden by shrubs. On impulse, he turned sharply, plunging them into darkness. Killing the lights, he parked behind a rocky outcropping.

They sat tensely, watching the main road. The SUV roared past without slowing.

Evan let out a breath. "Who are these people?"

Sarah shook her head, eyes haunted. "I don't know. But I have a feeling this is just the beginning."

Evan knew she was right. Their discovery at the dig had started something dangerous. And there was no turning back now.

Sarah's eyes narrowed as she watched Ramirez prowling around their office, his gaze raking over their research.

"You won't find anything useful here," she said sharply. "We already sent all our important data to a secure server."

Ramirez let out a mocking laugh. "Oh, I'm sure I can dig something up. Maybe tamper with a few things..." He picked up an ancient tablet and turned it over in his hands.

Evan tensed, exchanging an anxious look with Sarah. They couldn't let Ramirez sabotage months of detailed research.

Thinking fast, Sarah grabbed a random journal off the desk and waved it at Ramirez. "You know, I did find something odd in my notes last night. A reference to a hidden antechamber we hadn't explored yet."

Ramirez's eyes gleamed with interest. Sarah had hooked him.

"Let me just grab my copy. I'll show you the passa ge..." She ducked behind a shelf, pretending to search through papers.

Evan caught on. As Ramirez watched Sarah, Evan quietly stuffed their most vital research into his bag: maps, journals, flash drives—anything Ramirez could use against them.

"Found it!" Sarah reemerged, holding a journal open to a random page. She pointed to a meaningless diagram, launching an elaborate deception about a secret chamber.

Evan slid his stuffed bag behind a filing cabinet. They'd outmaneuvered Ramirez for now. But the ruthless rival would be back. This was just the beginning of something far more dangerous.

Sarah droned on, weaving an intricate web of fake clues and mysteries about the supposed hidden chamber. Ramirez's eyes gleamed greedily as he leaned in, hanging on her every word.

Evan used the distraction to gather the last of their vital evidence and research discreetly. As he stuffed notebooks into his bag, his mind raced. Where could they go that Ramirez wouldn't find them? The institute was compromised. Nowhere here was safe anymore.

"We'll have to take this somewhere secure," Evan muttered to Sarah as she continued to string Ramirez. "Somewhere, he can't get to it."

Sarah nodded almost imperceptibly, still engrossed in spinning her complex tale.

Evan zipped up the stuffed bag and stashed it behind the filing cabinet with the others. He quickly gathered a few essentials—passports, cash, and plane tickets. Ramirez was cunning, and he would try to cut off their escape routes. They needed to get out fast.

"Well!" Evan roared, interrupting Sarah's endless monologue. "We better get going if we want to follow up on this lead." He shot Sarah a meaningful look.

"Oh yes, of course!" Sarah said, snapping the journal shut. "Let's hurry, this discovery won't wait!"

They rushed out the door, leaving a bewildered Ramirez in their dust. In the hallway, Sarah and Evan exchanged a knowing glance. The game was on. Ramirez would be right behind them, watching their every move.

They hurried out of the institute, bags stuffed with precious research slung over their shoulders. As they stepped onto the bustling street, the fine hairs on Evan's neck prickled. He sensed they were being followed. Someone was watching them - Ramirez's henchman, no doubt. The hunt was underway.

Evan grabbed Sarah's arm and quickened his pace, weaving through the crowded marketplace. Vendors hawked their wares in a racket and color, but all Evan could focus on was the feeling of eyes boring into his back.

"We're being followed," he murmured under his breath.

Sarah tensed but didn't turn around. "I know. Don't look back."

They hurried on, ducking down narrow alleyways, trying to lose their pursuer in the maze-like streets. Evan's heart pounded, adrenaline flooding his veins. He knew Ramirez would stop at nothing to beat them to the treasure.

Suddenly, Sarah pulled Evan into a narrow doorway, out of sight. He stumbled into a dusty shop filled with artifacts and relics. Sarah put a finger to her lips, gesturing for silence. They crouched down, hidden among the shelves.

Evan struggled to control his breathing, pulse racing. Footsteps echoed down the alley outside. After an agonizing minute, they faded into the distance.

"That was close," Sarah whispered. "But he'll be back. We need to get out of Cairo tonight."

Evan nodded, his mind racing. Ramirez had cut off the airport, so their only option was to travel overland across the desert through Bandit Country. It would be dangerous.

But the treasure - and human history - hung in the balance. They had to succeed.

"We'll take the night train south," Evan said decisively. "And disappear into the desert."

Sarah considered, then nodded. The game was on. And they couldn't afford to lose.

Sarah's mind whirred as she glanced around the dusty shop, taking in their surroundings. "We need disguises if we're going to make it to the train station without being spotted."

She rummaged through a pile of dusty robes and held up two traditional galabeyas. "Here, put this on." She tossed one to Evan.

He quickly shed his button-down shirt and cargo pants and pulled the long, flowing galabeya over his head. Sarah did the same, covering her hair with a scarf.

"Grab those walking sticks," she said, pointing to a barrel in the corner. Evan complied, handing one to her.

"Let's go." Sarah peered out the door. Dusk was falling over the busy Cairo streets. People rushed home before curfew. She stepped out, Evan on her heels. Blending into the crowd, they made their way through the bustling market. Evan resisted the urge to look over his shoulder, trusting Sarah's instincts.

As they navigated the maze of alleys, he noticed Sarah using the walking stick to check their six discreetly. He kept his head down. They were invisible in the sea of people - for now. But he knew Ramirez's men would be combing the city for them. The train station was still five blocks away.

Sarah tensed, leaning in close. "Black sedan. Ten o'clock."

Evan's pulse spiked. "Just keep walking," he murmured. "We're almost there."

The ancient walls of Cairo hid many dangers. But also many ways to disappear.

Sarah quickened her pace ever so slightly, gripping her walking stick. She could feel the sedan inching along behind them. Any moment now, their pursuers would make a move.

Evan matched her stride, his senses heightened. His mind raced through escape routes—alleys, rooftops, the crowded market. The train station glowed in the distance.

Just a few more steps...

The tires screeched as the sedan accelerated. Sarah whirled around, and the staff was ready. Four men spilled out, their faces obscured by kufiyas.

"Run!" she shouted.

Evan was already sprinting down the nearest alley. Sarah swung the staff at the nearest assailant and then turned on her heel. She raced after Evan, feet flying over the uneven cobblestones.

Shouts echoed behind them as their pursuers pursued them on foot. Evan careened around a corner and almost slammed into a produce stand. He vaulted over it, sending the fruit scattering.

"This way!" He tore down an even narrower alley. Sarah followed close behind. The sound of running feet was getting closer. She gripped her staff, ready to make a stand.

"Here!" Evan called. He had found a slender opening between two buildings. They slipped through just as their pursuers rounded the corner. Pressing themselves against the wall, they held their breath.

The men rushed by their hiding place. After a few heart-pounding moments, the footsteps faded into the distance.

Evan let out a sigh of relief. "Let's go, quick."

Staying in the shadows, they crept through Cairo's backstreets. The train station was close. But Ramirez's men would not give up the hunt so efficiently.

Sarah and Evan hurried through the winding alleys, watching for any sign of their pursuers. Adrenaline pumped through their veins even as their lungs burned from exertion.

Up ahead, the alley opened up into a small courtyard. Evan paused, peering around the corner. Seeing it empty, he waved Sarah forward.

They were halfway across the courtyard when a black sedan screeched to a halt, blocking their exit. Four men leaped out, rifles raised.

"End of the line," one growled in Arabic.

Sarah tightened her grip on her staff, ready to fight. But they were outgunned.

Evan's mind raced. Their research and their life's work were at stake, and he had to protect them.

"Wait!" he said, switching to Arabic. "We can make a deal."

The men looked to their leader, who motioned for Evan to continue.

"Our work is worth far more than you know," Evan improvised. "Help us escape, and you'll be rewarded beyond your wildest dreams."

The leader considered this. Evan held his breath.

Finally, the man nodded. "You have a deal. But cross us, and you die."

Evan let out a breath. Nodding to Sarah, they got in the sedan. As it sped away, Evan knew their troubles were far from over. But for now, they lived to fight another day.

Chapter 6

Evan sat hunched over his desk, surrounded by towering stacks of ancient scrolls and artifacts. The glow of his desk lamp illuminated a clay tablet in his hands. He brushed a layer of dust from its surface, revealing a series of intricate symbols etched into the clay.

"This is incredible, Sarah," Evan said, glancing up as his colleague entered the room. "I think we're finally making progress decoding these symbols."

Sarah strode over, her eyes bright with excitement. "I've made a breakthrough. Look at this."

She produced a small, flat tablet from her bag, presenting it to Evan with a flourish. He took it carefully, turning it over in his hands. The symbols looked familiar yet slightly different from the others they had uncovered.

His pulse quickened as his mind raced through translations. This was the clue they desperately needed—the final piece to unlock the secret location of the hidden treasure.

Evan's eyes darted back and forth between the two tablets, comparing the intricate carvings. He reached for a magnifying glass and peered closer at the new artifact. Sarah watched intently, her body tense with anticipation.

"I don't believe it," Evan murmured. "These markings are some map. We're going to find it, Sarah. The lost treasure is within our grasp!"

Sarah's eyes shone excitedly as she leaned in to examine the tablet more closely. "You're right; this looks just like the cartography we've seen in other artifacts from that period. See here?" She traced her finger along a series of symbols. "This has to indicate some kind of geographical location."

Evan nodded, his mind racing. "Which means this tablet must be a fragment of a larger map. One that could lead us right to the treasure if we can find the remaining pieces."

He rose from his desk, beginning to pace back and forth. Sarah watched him, knowing the wheels were turning in his brilliant mind.

"We need expert guidance if we're going to track down the rest of this map," Evan said, turning to Sarah. "I know just the man for the job. Dr. Aldridge at the university is the foremost expert on ancient Egyptian cartography. If anyone can help us interpret the meaning of this tablet, it's him."

Sarah tilted her head. "Do you think he can be trusted? This discovery needs to be handled delicately."

"Aldridge is eccentric, but he's got integrity," Evan replied. "I'd trust him with my life. And more importantly, with the location of this treasure."

Sarah considered this for a moment and then nodded firmly. "Okay then, let's pay him a visit tomorrow morning." She carefully placed the tablet back into her bag. "We're so close now. The treasure must be protected."

Evan clapped a hand on her shoulder. "We'll do it together. Our work is far from over, but for now...we celebrate!"

Their laughter echoed through the empty halls as they left the office, hope and determination fueling their search for answers. The treasure was within reach at last.

The following day, Evan and Sarah arrived at Dr. Aldridge's office. The space was cramped and cluttered, stacked with books, maps, and artifacts. As they entered, Dr. Aldridge emerged behind a towering pile of scrolls.

"Evan, my boy!" he exclaimed, shaking Evan's hand vigorously. Despite his disheveled appearance, Aldridge's eyes were alert and keen.

Evan made the introductions. "Dr. Aldridge, this is my colleague Dr. Sarah Johnson. Sarah, meet Dr. Horace Aldridge, an expert in all things ancient and Egyptian."

"A pleasure to meet you, Dr. Johnson," Aldridge said, shaking her hand. His grip was surprisingly firm for his slender frame.

Sarah studied the eccentric professor. Could they trust him with the knowledge of their discovery? She glanced at Evan, and he gave her a subtle nod.

"Please, call me Sarah," she replied politely.

Evan pulled the clay tablet from his bag. "Dr. Aldridge, Sarah, and I could use your expertise. We believe this tablet is a fragment of an ancient Egyptian map. Can you take a look and give us your assessment?"

Aldridge's eyes lit up at the sight of the artifact. He turned it over delicately in his weathered hands, scrutinizing every detail.

"Remarkable, simply remarkable," he murmured. He set the tablet down and rifled through a stack of reference books. After cross-checking several sources, he looked up at Evan and Sarah.

"You were right to come to me. This is indeed a fragment of a larger cartographic work. If my hunch is correct, the full map could lead you to Tutankhamun's long-lost treasure."

Evan and Sarah exchanged an excited glance. The treasure was within reach! But first, they needed to reassemble the map.

Sarah leaned forward eagerly. "Do you know where we can find the other pieces?"

Aldridge's eyes twinkled behind his spectacles. " I just might. I've heard rumors that a collector in Cairo recently acquired a similar tablet at auction."

He jotted down a name and address. "Start there. I'll call and see what else I can dig up."

Evan clasped Aldridge's arm. "We're in your debt, Doctor. Your expertise could prove invaluable."

Over the next few weeks, Evan and Sarah crisscrossed the globe, tracking down leads on the map fragments.

In the stuffy backroom of an antiquities shop in Cairo, they outbid a ruthless competitor to purchase a crucial piece. Later, in the Hermitage Museum's vaults, they used Aldridge's credentials to access another fragment mislabeled as a Sumerian relic.

Their search led them through Paris's salons, Morocco's markets, and even to a secretive collector in

Shanghai. Each new fragment brought them closer to completing the map.

But other parties were after the map as well. In Istanbul, Evan and Sarah were ambushed outside a bazaar by a band of armed thieves looking to steal their fragments. Only Sarah's quick reflexes and martial arts skills allowed them to escape unharmed.

The threat was clear - they had to complete the map before it fell into the wrong hands. The treasure - and fate of the world - hung in the balance.

The auction house in London was packed with eager buyers and shifty dealers. Evan and Sarah sat near the front, anxiously awaiting the next lot.

"Lot 117, a fragment of an ancient clay tablet etched with undeciphered symbols," the auctioneer announced.

The bidding started slowly but soon shot upwards as Evan, Sarah, and a smartly dressed woman across the room engaged in a heated war of bids.

"We can't let her get this piece," Evan whispered to Sarah. "It's too important."

Sarah nodded, her eyes fixed on their rival. She scratched her nose - their prearranged signal - and Evan upped their max bid.

The price climbed higher and higher until, finally, the bang of the gavel signaled their narrow victory. They had secured the fragment but at a steep cost.

Evan carefully fits the new fragment into the map in their hotel room. More details emerge on the faded clay, including the outline of a mountain and a winding river.

"We're getting close," he murmured. "If we can just stay ahead of the others..."

Sarah squeezed his shoulder. "We will. This treasure is meant for us to find and protect. I can feel it."

Evan hoped she was right. The stakes grew higher with each new clue. But he knew that with Sarah by his side, they would prevail. The treasure called to them over land and sea. And they would answer its call.

Sarah's phone buzzed, breaking the silence. She read the text message, then turned to Evan.

"That was Dr. Carter. He says he's found a lead on the final piece."

Evan's eyes lit up. "Where is it?"

"A private collector in the Amazon jungle. Getting it won't be easy."

Sarah traced her finger along the incomplete map. "We have to try. This is our chance to finish what we started."

Evan nodded, his expression serious. "Then we leave tonight."

They packed light and flew to Manaus, Brazil. A supply plane took them further into the rainforest until they stood at the jungle's edge.

"Stay close," Evan said. "These trees can swallow you whole."

They hacked through the dense undergrowth, following a narrow trail. Strange cries echoed around them, and unseen creatures rustled the leaves.

When the path forked, Evan consulted the map fragment. He pointed left. "This way."

Soon, they reached a fast-flowing river. An ancient rope bridge stretched across the churning water. Sarah paled but bravely stepped forward.

Halfway across, a board cracked under her foot. She cried out as her leg plunged through. Clinging to the ropes, she looked at Evan with frightened eyes.

"Don't move! I'm coming!" He crawled towards her along the swaying bridge. Gripping her arms, he pulled her to safety.

They collapsed in each other's arms on the far bank, hearts pounding. Then, driven by purpose, they plunged onward into the steamy jungle. The final piece awaited them.

Evan and Sarah pushed through the dense jungle, following the winding trail marked on their map fragment.

The air hung heavy and humid, and unseen creatures chittered in the canopy above.

Rounding a bend, they came upon a clearing. A cliff face loomed before them, vines cascading down its face. Ancient carvings were etched into the weathered stone.

"This is it," Evan said, consulting the map. "The final piece must be hidden somewhere on that cliff."

They searched the base, finding small niches and openings half-concealed by vegetation. Crawling on hands and knees, they explored every nook and cranny.

"Here!" Sarah called out. She uncovered a small bundle wrapped in fraying cloth in a narrow crevice. Her hands trembled, and she unfolded it, revealing the last fragment of the map.

"We did it," Evan breathed. "Now, let's get out of here."

They turned to go but found their path blocked by three men wielding machetes. Bandits.

"Hand over the map," one growled.

Evan stepped protectively in front of Sarah. "Run," he whispered.

As she fled, he launched himself at the men. They clashed in a flurry of fists and blades. Evan took a slice to his arm but managed to disarm one bandit.

A gunshot rang out. Sarah stood with a smoking pistol. The men scattered, one wounded.

Reunited, Evan and Sarah leaned against each other in exhaustion and relief. The final piece was theirs. Now, to find the hidden treasure.

Chapter 7

The computer screen's glow illuminated Evan's face as he stared intently at the ancient symbols scrolling past. "I've done it," he whispered.

Sarah glanced up from the crumbling scroll laid out on the table. "Done what?"

"Cracked section twelve." Evan's eyes shone with excitement behind his glasses. "I finally deciphered the repeated glyph sequence."

"Let me see." Sarah moved to peer over Evan's shoulder, keen to examine his breakthrough. Her mind whirred, and she was already running through analytical processes to verify his discovery.

Evan tapped the screen. "Here, look. This symbol keeps appearing but with slight variations. I think it's some key or codex."

Studying the screen, Sarah compared the highlighted symbols. Evan was right; the similarities were too precise to be coincidental. It had to be significant.

"Good catch." She squeezed his shoulder, her pride swelling. They were one step closer to unraveling this ancient mystery.

Evan grinned, exhaustion forgotten in the thrill of revelation. "With this, we might finally crack the next section. All those late nights paid off."

Sarah nodded, thoughts turning to the endless hours spent deciphering esoteric clues. She lived for this - the joy of discovery, of revealing secrets lost to time. There was still a long road ahead, but with Evan, she knew they would unravel it together.

Sarah's mind raced ahead, considering how to leverage Evan's breakthrough. Based on this newly revealed codex, she had to provide more clues. Her gaze drifted over their lab, cluttered with artifacts and research.

"We should re-examine everything with fresh eyes," she said. "Now that we can recognize this symbol's significance, who knows what connections we'll find."

Evan nodded, following her train of thought. "I'll start compiling a list of relevant items." He moved towards a storage shelf, already mentally cataloging its contents.

Sarah returned her focus to the scroll, hoping to uncover more coded repetitions. But her concentration kept wandering, and she was eager to make discoveries.

Evan called out, "Sarah, look at this!"

She saw him holding a small golden amulet adorned with familiar glyphs. "It's the same symbol sequence," he exclaimed. "This changes everything!"

Reverently, Sarah took the amulet, marveling at the intricate craftsmanship. She traced the tiny symbols with a fingertip. Here, finally, was tangible proof of their theories.

"With this, we can confirm the codex," she murmured. "It unlocks the next layer of messages." Excitement thrummed through her.

"We should compare it to other artifacts, find more connections," Evan suggested, pacing around the room. He paused before an ancient vase. "Maybe patterns will emerge, clues about its purpose."

Sarah agreed. They had to mine every scrap of context to decipher the amulet's significance.

"Let's document everything meticulously," she said, grabbing her camera. The thrill of discovery had her heart racing. With focus and teamwork, the secrets of the past were finally within reach.

Hours later, bleary-eyed and stiff from hunching over artifacts, Evan straightened with a groan. He removed his glasses and rubbed his eyes.

"This is maddening," he muttered. "We're no closer to answers."

Sarah glanced up from an ancient tablet she was examining under a magnifying glass. "There has to be something we missed," she said.

Evan turned slowly, gazing around the room. His eyes landed on a fragmentary mural tucked in a far corner. Drawn to it, he stepped closer, intrigued by the faded images.

"Sarah, look." He pointed to a figure depicted holding a similar amulet. "This seems to be a ceremony of some kind."

Joining him, Sarah studied the mural intently. "You're right; this could be significant." She retrieved her camera to document the find.

"If we cross-reference this with the codex..." Evan hurried back to the scrolls scattered across the table. Sarah followed, pulse quickening.

They immediately noticed correlations between the mural's symbols and the code's cryptic repetitions.

"A connection," breathed Sarah. "This is too aligned to be a coincidence."

Evan nodded, mind racing. "The amulet must be central to deciphering the messages."

Their eyes met, alight with exhilaration. Each new revelation fueled their enthusiasm. The secrets of the past were yielding, slowly but surely, to their tenacity.

Sarah's eyes narrowed as she studied the amulet, turning it over carefully in her hands. The golden disc was adorned with intricate symbols and delicate filigree work along the edges. She ran her fingers over the surface, feeling for any irregularities.

"There must be more to this," she murmured.

Evan leaned in, equally engrossed in examining the artifact. "Look here," he said, pointing to a tiny glyph along the rim. "This marking is repeated in the codex."

Sarah retrieved the ancient scroll and compared the two symbols. "You're right. It's an exact match."

Her brow furrowed as she scrutinized the amulet further. The metal seemed to give slightly under her probing fingers along the bottom edge.

"Wait, I think..." She deftly pressed and slid a hidden panel along the rim. It clicked open to reveal a tiny compartment inside.

"A secret chamber!" exclaimed Evan.

Nestled within was a tightly rolled parchment, yellowed with age. Sarah gingerly removed it, her hands trembling with excitement. As the parchment uncurled, it revealed a series of hieroglyphs.

"This must be the key," she breathed. "It's just like the codex."

Evan's eyes shone as he studied the symbols. "If we can translate this, it may unlock everything."

With painstaking care, they began cross-referencing the parchment with the scrolls, deciphering meaning from the intricate glyphs. Each correlation brought them closer to unraveling the ancient messages.

"The answers are within our grasp," said Evan, hope and determination etched on his face.

Sarah met his gaze, knowing that soon, their dedication would unveil secrets lost to time. The past was revealing itself, one precious symbol at a time.

Evan and Sarah worked late into the night, fueled by adrenaline and the promise of revelation. Hieroglyphs swam before their eyes as they traced connections between the newly discovered parchment and the cryptic codex.

With each correlation made, more of the code's veil lifted. Like excavating an ancient site one brushstroke at a time, the hidden messages emerged.

"Look here," said Sarah, holding a magnifying glass over the scrolls. "This sequence links to the amulet's inscription."

Evan nodded, scribbling notes furiously. "You're right. It's a perfect match."

Their expertise unfurled the code's tightly wound secrets piece by piece. Having devoted years to studying these lost languages, Sarah and Evan found familiarity in the intricate symbols, and meaning blossomed under their scrutiny.

But as morning light crept across the scroll-strewn table, frustration crept in. Details eluded them, passages left undeciphered. Each step forward revealed ten more hidden.

Evan pushed his glasses up, rubbing gritty eyes. "There must be something we're missing."

"We've tried every combination," Sarah sighed, winding a lock of hair around her finger.

"What if we're interpreting it wrong? Let's go over the amulet again."

They stifled yawns as they reviewed their notes, searching for flaws. The code refused to surrender fully, keeping its secrets close. Still, Sarah and Evan persevered, determined to unravel the ancient mystery.

Sarah leaned back, stretching her tired limbs. As her eyes scanned the scrolls again, one symbol caught her attention.

"Wait...look at this," she said, jabbing her finger at the parchment. "This marking is different."

Evan peered closer, adjusting his glasses. "You're right; it's subtly altered. How did we miss that before?"

Sarah shook her head, already grabbing reference materials to cross-check. "It must be a clue. A way to unlock the next section."

Evan's excitement grew as Sarah worked. He watched her make notes, muttering theories under her breath as she pieced together connections.

"Got it," she finally announced. "It's a code within the code. This variant points to a hidden message."

"Brilliant!" Evan exclaimed. "Let's incorporate that into our translation."

They dove back in with renewed vigor, energized by the breakthrough. The code slowly surrendered its secrets under their expertise, hinting at revelations to come.

Evan and Sarah looked determined as the sun rose over the distant pyramids, bathing the room in light. Though the code remained unfinished, its core had begun to unravel. They were close, so close, to a crucial truth buried for millennia.

Their journey was far from over, but with each discovery, they drew nearer to their ultimate goal—illuminating the past. The future shimmered with potential, and mysteries waited to be unearthed.

Chapter 8

The flickering light of Evan's torch cast eerie shadows across the ancient hieroglyphics etched into the tomb walls. He ran his fingers over the intricate carvings, brow furrowed in concentration as he tried to decipher their meaning.

"Any luck?" Sarah asked, peering down at the weathered papyrus scroll in her hands.

"Not yet," Evan sighed. "This code is incredibly complex."

Footsteps echoed from the passage ahead. Evan and Sarah exchanged a wary glance, muscles tensing. A figure emerged from the darkness - a man in his 40s with neatly combed brown hair and wire-rimmed glasses.

"Hello there!" he said brightly, extending a hand in greeting. "Dr. Michael Barnes. I'm an archaeologist exploring these ruins as well."

Evan studied him critically before shaking his hand. Sarah nodded in greeting, guarded.

"I'm Dr. Evan Reynolds, and this is my colleague, Dr. Sarah Johnson," Evan introduced himself. "It's a pleasure to meet you, Dr. Barnes. If you know ancient Egyptian languages, we could help decipher this cryptic text."

"What a coincidence - ancient languages are my specialty!" Barnes said enthusiastically. "Here, let me take a look."

He joined Evan at the wall, peering closely at the symbols. As he studied them, Sarah watched Barnes out of her eye, searching for any sign of deception. But the man seemed wholly absorbed in translating the code, muttering under his breath.

For now, he appeared sincere in his offer of help. However, only time will tell if Dr. Michael Barnes can be trusted.

Sarah's eyes narrowed as Barnes pointed to a section of hieroglyphs.

"This symbol represents the sound 'DJ.' So, this word might be 'diesel,'" he explained.

Evan nodded eagerly as Barnes continued deciphering, seemingly impressed with the man's knowledge. But Sarah noticed Barnes hesitated briefly when identifying one of the symbols. She made a mental note of it.

"With your help, Dr. Barnes, I think we're finally making progress on cracking this code," Evan said excitedly.

"Happy to lend my expertise," Barnes replied with a smile. "Why don't we take a break? You two must be famished."

He pulled some energy bars from his pack and offered them around. Evan readily accepted one, but Sarah waved it off, not taking her eyes off Barnes.

As the two men ate, Barnes asked about their research, probing for details. Evan openly shared, but Sarah remained tight-lipped. Something about Barnes' overly helpful demeanor seemed off, and she couldn't shake the feeling he was hiding his true intentions.

Sarah sidled beside Evan as Barnes pretended to examine some artifacts across the tomb.

"Something's not right with him," she whispered. "Did you notice how he hesitated on that symbol?"

Evan furrowed his brow. "You think he intentionally misidentified it?"

"Maybe. Or he's not as knowledgeable as he claims."

Barnes suddenly turned back towards them, and Sarah fell silent.

"Fascinating carvings over here," he remarked, beckoning them over. "Remarkably well-preserved."

As they inspected the carvings, Barnes reached towards Evan's notebook, left open on a crate. Before

Sarah could stop him, Barnes spilled water from his canteen onto the pages.

"Oh dear, how clumsy of me!" Barnes exclaimed. "I'm sorry about that."

Evan frowned as the ink bled across his meticulous notes.

When Barnes moved away again, Sarah confronted Evan in hushed tones. "Did you see that? He ruined your notebook on purpose."

Evan hesitated. "I'm not sure...it could've been an accident."

Sarah shook her head firmly. "He's sabotaging us, Evan. We can't trust him."

Evan sighed, conflicted. But the evidence was mounting against Barnes—one too many inconsistencies.

They'd have to be cautious about sharing information with the man and closely monitor their artifacts.

Sarah's suspicions were confirmed when she caught Dr. Barnes slipping the gold scarab amulet into his pocket. The amulet was a key to deciphering the code they had been working tirelessly to crack.

"Don't move," Sarah said sternly, stepping out from the shadows.

Barnes froze his hand, still in his pocket, gripping the amulet. His eyes narrowed.

"I knew you were up to no good," Sarah continued. "Hand it over, now."

Evan emerged behind Sarah, his expression hard. "You've betrayed our trust, Dr. Barnes. We treated you as a colleague. Explain yourself."

Barnes hesitated, then slowly removed the amulet from his pocket. "You're right; I haven't been frank with you," he said. "But you must understand. There are powerful forces at work here that neither of you can begin to comprehend."

"Don't give us that cryptic nonsense," Evan snapped, grabbing the amulet from Barnes' hand. "We asked you to assist us as a fellow academic, not steal priceless artifacts."

"Please, let me explain," Barnes pleaded. "I'm not who you think I am. I was sent here undercover by a covert organization. They want me to retrieve the treasure for them by any means necessary. I wish there were another way."

Sarah scoffed. "Right, like we're going to believe that. You're just a common thief."

Evan stepped forward threateningly. "We should report him to the authorities right away."

Barnes raised his hands. "You have every right to do so. But consider this: How do you think these powerful forces will react when their agent fails to deliver? Your lives could be in grave danger."

Evan and Sarah exchanged uneasy glances, unsure whether to trust Barnes' warning.

Sarah turned to Evan, lowering her voice. "What should we do? Can we trust anything he says?"

Evan shook his head, conflicted. "I don't know. This changes everything."

He looked back at Barnes. "Even if you're saying it is true, we can't simply hand over these priceless artifacts. There must be another way."

Barnes' expression was grave. "I'm afraid you have no choice. I wish I could have been honest with you from the start. But they were watching my every move. I had my orders."

Sarah crossed her arms. "That's not good enough. You betrayed our trust, no matter your reasons." She looked at Evan. "We need to contact the authorities and get out of here with the artifacts."

Evan hesitated, thinking it through. Handing Barnes over could put them directly in the crosshairs of this sinister organization. And yet, simply giving up the artifacts was unthinkable.

"Sarah's right," he said finally. "We must protect these treasures, no matter the risk to ourselves." He met

Barnes' gaze. "I'm sorry, but we can't allow you to take them."

Barnes' shoulders slumped in resignation. "I understand. I truly am sorry for the position I've put you both in." He held out his wrists. "Do what you must."

Evan pulled out his satellite phone, ready to call for help. But they still faced an impossible choice, with no clear path ahead. The web of deceit had only grown more complex.

Sarah paced the small antechamber, her mind racing. They were in grave danger, but the authorities could be hours away. She glanced at Evan, who was still on the phone requesting backup and transportation. His voice was steady, but she could see the tension in his shoulders.

"We need to move now," she said when he ended the call. "I don't trust Barnes not to have alerted his contacts. Staying here makes us sitting ducks."

Evan nodded. "Agreed. We should take what we can carry and find a more defensible position." He moved swiftly, gathering scrolls and minor artifacts into his pack.

Sarah did the same, and all her senses were on high alert. Her pistol felt reassuringly heavy on her hip, and she had no qualms about using it if needed.

Barnes sat silently against the wall, appearing resigned, but she didn't trust him for a second. His allegiances were divided.

"Let's go," Evan said, swinging his pack over his shoulder. He kept a wary eye on Barnes as they exited the antechamber.

The twisting tunnels of the tomb were like a maze. Sarah tracked each turn, etching a mental map. A wrong move could trap them indefinitely. She strained to hear any sounds of pursuit over their echoing footsteps.

"Do you think we can make it out before they arrive?" she asked Evan in a low voice.

"It'll be close," he said. "But we have the advantage of knowing the layout. I hope luck is on our side."

Sarah nodded, wishing she had shared his optimism. But she knew their trials were far from over. The past riddles were nothing compared to the deadly secrets they now carried.

Chapter 9

As Evan and Sarah stepped into the temple's inner chamber, the air was thick with dust and the musk of antiquity. Evan could barely contain his excitement, his heart pounding as his eyes adjusted to the dim light. Ancient hieroglyphs and carvings adorning every surface emerged from the shadows.

"This is it," he whispered. "If the clue is here, this room may hold the key."

Sarah nodded, her eagerness evident in her quickened breathing. They began examining the walls methodically, inspecting each symbol and motif. Evan traced his fingers over the intricate carvings, his mind racing.

"Look there," Sarah said, pointing to a section near the back. Evan crossed the chamber in long strides. "See that symbol, the one that looks like an eye?"

Evan peered closer. "Yes, that's the Eye of Horus. It represents healing and protection."

"Right. But see how it connects to the others?" Sarah followed the intricate pattern with her finger. "It's like they form a map, with the Eye at the center."

Evan's pulse quickened. "A map to the treasure," he whispered. "Sarah, I think you've found it!"

Sarah smiled, but her eyes remained focused, scanning the walls. "We're close; I can feel it. The clue must be here somewhere..."

Evan squeezed her shoulder, his pride swelling in his chest. They were one step closer to unraveling history's greatest mystery, and with Sarah's brilliant mind, he had no doubt they would succeed.

Sarah's gaze landed on a darkened corner of the chamber. Squinting, she could make out the faint glint of something metallic.

"Over there," she said, grabbing Evan's arm. They rushed to the corner, flashlights in hand. Wedged into a crevice in the crumbling wall was a small metal object. Gingerly, Evan reached in and extracted it, brushing away cobwebs and sand.

It was an ornate bronze key about six inches long. Intricate hieroglyphs and symbols decorated its bow and shaft. Sarah's brow furrowed as she studied it closely under her flashlight.

"This is ancient Egyptian," she murmured. "See the ankhs and scarabs? They symbolize life and rebirth."

Evan turned the key over in his hands, pulse quickening. "You're right. This must be thousands of years old." He met Sarah's gaze. "It's no ordinary key. This has to unlock something critical."

Sarah nodded, mind racing. "A hidden chamber or a chest containing the next puzzle piece." Her eyes shone with excitement.

Evan grinned. "Well, there's only one way to find out." Gripping the key tightly, he scanned the shadowy chamber. "Let's start looking for a lock."

Sarah methodically swept her flashlight over the chamber walls, searching for cracks or crevices that might indicate a hidden compartment. Ancient sites like this often had secret rooms concealed behind walls.

Evan did the same on the opposite side, running his fingers over the stone, looking for any irregularities. His heart pounded with anticipation. They were so close, he could feel it.

After several minutes, Evan's flashlight glinted off something on the back wall - thin grooves in the stone barely visible beneath layers of dust and grime.

"Sarah, look at this," he said. She hurried over.

"It's a door," she breathed, tracing the outline with her finger. "And look - there's a tiny keyhole."

Evan inserted the ornate key with a steady hand. It slid smoothly into place. He glanced at Sarah, eyes bright.

"Here we go."

He took a breath and turned the key. At first, nothing happened. Then, with a grind of stone on stone, part of the wall swung slowly inward.

Beyond lay darkness. Gripping their flashlights, Evan and Sarah stepped into the void. The air was heavy with mystery and the promise of revelations to come.

Sarah swept her flashlight over the chamber, which was revealed behind the hidden door. Ancient scrolls and clay tablets covered every surface, layered in centuries of undisturbed dust. Her eyes went wide.

"It's a treasure trove," she whispered. "These must be centuries old."

Evan picked up a scroll gingerly, hands trembling. As he unrolled it, his breath caught.

"Sarah, these are written in the ancient language we've been deciphering in the codex!"

She hurried over to look, scanning the intricate symbols inked onto the aged parchment. "You're right," she murmured. "This could be the key to unlocking the next step in finding the treasure."

Working quickly but carefully, they began gathering scrolls, notebooks, and tablets, searching for anything that might relate to the codex or help interpret its hidden messages. Each new artifact felt like a step closer to unraveling the mystery that had consumed them for months.

Evan's mind raced as he tried to absorb the knowledge these writings, written by ancient hands centuries ago, contained. What secrets did they hold? What revelations about a culture lost to time did they include? He had to suppress his urge to stop and study each new find; knowing speed was critical with potential pursuers on their trail.

"We need to get these back for analysis," Sarah said, echoing his thoughts as she packed her suitcase with priceless artifacts. "If we can decipher them, they could finally lead us to the treasure."

Evan nodded, hands full. "Let's move quickly. We're running out of time."

Sarah's eyes scanned the chamber, looking for anything they missed. She spotted a large object propped against the wall in the far corner, covered in cobwebs. Brushing away the dust, she revealed it to be an ornate chest.

"Evan, help me with this," she called. Together, they lifted the heavy chest, blowing off layers of grit. Evan fumbled with the rusty latch until the lid creaked open. Inside lay a pile of scrolls bound in leather cord.

Evan lifted one out with eager hands, carefully unrolling the cracked parchment. His eyes widened. "It's a map," he breathed.

Sarah peered over his shoulder. The map was intricately detailed, showing a vast desert landscape marked with cryptic symbols and annotations in the ancient script.

"Look, these landmarks match the ones referenced in the codex," Sarah said excitedly, tracing her finger along the map's features. Evan studied the intricate web of connections, picturing the described locations in his mind's eye.

"You're right. This map must indicate the directions to the next step in finding the treasure," he murmured. "We need to decipher exactly where this map is leading us."

Kneeling on the dusty floor, the two pored over the map, scribbling notes and cross-referencing their decodes, their faces alight with purpose. Piece by piece, they began assembling a path, compelled forward by the promise of discovery.

"If we follow this correctly, it seems the map indicates a specific oasis here," Evan finally said, tapping his pencil.

Sarah nodded. "Then that's our next destination." She carefully rolled up the map. "Let's move."

Sarah tucked the map into her pack as they stood. Dust motes danced in the shafts of light piercing the darkened chamber. Evan took one last sweeping look at the room that had yielded such a vital clue.

"Hard to believe this has been hidden here all these centuries," he murmured.

Sarah nodded, resting a hand on the wall. "Let's hope we're meant to uncover its secrets finally."

With a last lingering look, they turned and headed for the exit. Evan pulled up short as they stepped out into the blazing desert sunlight.

"Get down!" he hissed, yanking Sarah behind a crumbling wall. Peering out, they saw a convoy of black vehicles approaching, armed men emerging.

Sarah's eyes hardened. "It's Anton Voronov's men. They must have followed us here."

Evan gritted his teeth. Of course, the power-hungry tycoon was after the treasure, too. "We can't let them beat us to it. We need to slip away unnoticed."

Sarah nodded, eyes darting, assessing options. "There's some coverage leading toward that ravine. We can use it to circle behind and make a break for the jeeps."

They moved swiftly, using the terrain like shadows. As they slid into the driver's seat, hearts hammered with exhilaration and purpose. The engines roared to life, speeding them toward answers hidden within the endless dunes.

Sarah's foot slammed the gas pedal, pebbles spraying as the jeep fishtailed onto the desert road. In the rearview mirror, she saw two of Voronov's vehicles peel off in pursuit.

"Faster!" Evan urged. He twisted around, watching their pursuers gain ground at an alarming rate. Gritting his teeth, he turned back just as Sarah yanked the wheel, the jeep lurching down a side road.

"We can lose them in the village up ahead," she shouted over the engine's roar.

The battered buildings rose quickly, a maze of narrow alleys and sun-baked clay walls. Sarah navigated expertly, tires screeching as she whipped them around tight corners. Evan braced himself, one hand on the roll bar as they jolted down the cramped side streets.

Glancing back again, he saw one jeep clip a building as it struggled to keep pace. "It's working! Just a little farther..."

Suddenly, they burst into a crowded marketplace, vendors and shoppers scrambling out of their path. Sarah slammed the brakes, bringing them skidding to a stop behind some stalls. They killed the engine and crouched low as the enemy vehicles roared past.

Evan let out a shaky breath, adrenaline still surging. "That was close."

Sarah nodded, eyes alert. "But we're not out of this yet. We need to keep moving before they double back."

With that, they were off again, melting into the bazaar's chaos as they steadily escaped.

Sarah led the way as they slipped through the crowded marketplace, weaving between merchants and shoppers. Evan stayed close, keeping a wary eye out for any sign of their pursuers. His shirt stuck to his back with nervous sweat, his heart still pounding from the chase.

After what felt like an eternity of pressing through the crush of bodies, Sarah pulled Evan down a narrow alley, the din of the bazaar fading behind them. She paused, peering around a corner before waving him onward.

They emerged into a small, shaded courtyard, the high walls muffling the surrounding city's noise. Evan's shoulders sagged with relief. He felt he could breathe for the first time since spotting those jeeps.

"We should be safe here for now," Sarah said, leaning against the rough clay wall.

Evan nodded, swiping a hand across his brow. His mind raced, trying to make sense of what just happened. "They must have followed us from the temple. But how did they know?"

Sarah's eyes narrowed, her expression grim. "I don't know. But someone sold us out."

Evan sighed, knowing she was right. He began pacing the courtyard, adrenaline still buzzing through him. "We need to figure out our next move. The clock's ticking if they're onto us already."

"Agreed," Sarah said. She moved to the courtyard's center, spreading the map they'd found across an old stone bench. "If we're going to stay ahead of them, we must keep following the clues."

Evan joined her, peering down at the intricate symbols and landmarks depicted on the ancient parchment. Anticipation stirred within him as their quest for answers continued.

Chapter 10

Eerie shadows danced across the stone walls as Evan stared into the flickering flame of the oil lamp. His mind raced as he ran his fingers over the cracked edges of the ancient scroll on the table before him. What secrets did it contain? And, more importantly, would revealing them bring him the recognition he so desperately craved?

A shuffling of papers broke the heavy silence. Evan glanced up to see Sarah hunched over a stack of books, brow furrowed in concentration. He envied her tireless dedication, driven only by a desire to preserve history, not personal gain.

Evan sighed and adjusted his glasses. "Any luck over there?"

Sarah shook her head. "I can't make heads or tails of this cipher. The letters seem completely random."

"Let me take a look." Evan joined her at the table and examined the cryptic passages. Each symbol taunted him, daring his intellect to decipher their meaning.

Sarah leaned back, arms crossed. "What do you think? Dead end?"

Evan traced the strange markings; whispers of understanding tickled his mind. "Not yet. I think I'm starting to see a pattern here. Hand me that codex."

Sarah passed the weathered book to him. Evan's pulse quickened as his analytical skills engaged like gears in a machine—the symbols aligned into familiar shapes: a bird, an eye, a Sun.

"It's hieroglyphic," he muttered. "But altered...a code within the code."

Sarah perked up. "Can you crack it?"

Evan grinned. The thrill of discovery coursed through him. "Just watch me."

Sarah watched as Evan became absorbed in deciphering the code, his earlier doubts fading away. She envied his single-minded focus. While Evan was driven by intellectual curiosity, her motivations were more complex.

Yes, she wanted to preserve this lost history and culture, ensuring greedy collectors or corporations didn't monopolize its knowledge. But she wondered if her desire to protect the treasure from misuse clouded her judgment. Were they even entitled to its secrets?

"Have you considered..." Sarah began hesitantly, "That maybe this treasure wasn't meant to be found?"

Evan didn't look up, scribbling notes furiously. "Don't be absurd. Discovery expands human knowledge."

Sarah frowned. "But at what cost? Just because we find something doesn't mean we have the right to it."

"You can't stop progress in the name of cultural sensitivity," Evan scoffed.

"And you can't plunder ancient secrets out of ego!" Sarah shot back, rising to her feet.

Evan finally met her gaze, eyes blazing. "So I should leave this treasure to be pillaged by raiders and hoarded by billionaires? Is that what you want?"

"Of course not," Sarah said. "I just think we should consider the original creators' intentions."

Evan removed his glasses, pinching the bridge of his nose. "Sarah, I know your heart's in the right place. But we must uncover the past. What matters is how we use our knowledge after."

Sarah pondered this. Perhaps they could find a compromise between preservation and revelation. But only if they trusted each other's motives completely. And right now, Sarah wasn't sure if that trust existed.

Sarah's doubts lingered as she stared at the ancient codex. Its mysteries taunted her, symbols swimming before her eyes.

Beside her, Evan muttered under his breath, scribbling possibilities into his notebook. His focus was unbroken, even after their heated exchange.

Sarah sighed, returning her attention to the codex. As she examined it again, a previously unnoticed etching in the margin caught her eye. It was a tiny pictogram of a scarab beetle, barely visible against the faded papyrus.

"Evan, look at this," she said urgently. "Could this be a clue about the code?"

Evan's head snapped up. He leaned in close to inspect the scarab symbol, eyes brightening.

"You might be onto something," he murmured. "Scarabs were used to represent rebirth and the sun god Ra. Perhaps it's linked to the summer solstice?"

Sarah's pulse quickened. "Of course! Many ancient languages used solar references as codes. This could be the key to deciphering it."

A smile broke across Evan's face. "Sarah, you're brilliant! With this, I think we can finally crack the code."

All thoughts of their earlier disagreement faded away. Now, a shared purpose drove them, carried on waves of exhilaration. The answers were within reach at last.

Together, they dove back into the codex with renewed vigor. All doubts were banished. The only thing that mattered was their quest for knowledge and the promise of revelation glowing on the horizon.

Sarah's hands trembled as she turned the ancient papyrus pages, scanning for more clues. The scarab symbol unlocked new meanings in the cryptic glyphs and numerals before her.

"Here, look at this sequence," she said. "I think these numbers may correspond to dates on the Egyptian calendar related to the solstice."

Evan nodded, his eyes bright. "Yes, yes, you might be right!" He grabbed his notebook, flipping through pages of scribbled notes. "If we convert them to the Gregorian calendar, it could give us a precise location."

He began scratching out calculations, brow furrowed in concentration. Sarah leaned in beside him, one hand resting lightly on his shoulder. She could feel his muscles tense with excitement under her fingertips.

At that moment, nothing else existed except the two of them and the ancient code unfurling its secrets before their eyes. Evan's cologne mingled with the musty scent of parchment and clay in the air. Somewhere in the distance, a clock ticked away the seconds.

"Almost have it," Evan muttered. With a final flourish, he circled a sequence of numbers and letters.

Sarah caught her breath. "Are those..."

"Coordinates," Evan finished, meeting her widened eyes. "To the location of the treasure."

For a heartbeat, neither of them moved. The implications sank in. Then Evan broke into a grin of pure exhilaration.

"We did it!" He pulled Sarah into an impulsive embrace. She laughed aloud, relief and anticipation surging through her. The treasure was within their grasp at last!

Sarah's joy quickly faded as doubt crept in. She pulled back from Evan's embrace, her smile disappearing.

"Wait. How can we be sure this is right?" She traced the coordinates with one finger. "We could be misinterpreting something."

Evan's grin faded. He sat back, deflated. "You're right. I got carried away." He removed his glasses and rubbed his eyes. "There are a dozen ways we could be wrong."

Sarah began pacing, arms crossed. "We need to go over everything again from the start. Recheck every calculation."

Evan nodded grimly. He knew Sarah was right to be cautious, but it was difficult to rein in his impatience after coming so close.

They worked in determined silence, reexamining every scrap of evidence. The code has artifacts, star charts, and cryptic symbols. Hours they slipped by as they lost themselves in their task.

At last, Sarah tossed down her notebook in frustration. "It's no use. We're missing something."

Evan slammed a book shut. "There must be some clue we've overlooked." He hesitated. "Or maybe this is as far as we can take it with what we have."

Sarah turned to him, eyes flashing. "So, what, we just give up?"

"Of course not." Evan met her gaze steadily. "We keep trying. We've come too far to back down now."

Sarah let out a long breath, shoulders slumping. "You're right. We can do this." She managed a faint smile. "Whatever it takes."

Evan clasped her hand firmly. They would unravel this code yet. The treasure awaited them—they had to be patient and persistent to claim it.

Sarah's eyes suddenly lit up. "Wait a minute...what if we've been looking at this all wrong?"

She grabbed a star chart, tracing her finger along the constellations. "We kept assuming this was a map, but what if it's something more?"

Evan studied the chart intently. Realization dawned. "A code. The stars are the key to the code."

Sarah nodded, breathless. "Look, the brightest stars match these symbols." She indicated the mysterious markings throughout the ancient text.

Together, they worked feverishly to break the code using the stars as their cipher. The symbols slowly revealed letters, then words.

"Almost there," Evan muttered, scribbling furiously.

After agonizing minutes, they sat back, stunned. The message was complete.

"We did it," Sarah whispered, meeting Evan's wide-eyed gaze.

Evan let out a shaky laugh. "I can't believe it. We finally cracked the code."

They took a moment to let it sink in. Then Sarah picked up the deciphered message and read aloud. The lyrical words described a fabled treasure beyond imagination, hidden in a secret tomb deep beneath the sands.

Evan and Sarah exchanged an electrified look. The treasure's location was within their grasp. This changed everything.

"What now?" Sarah asked breathlessly.

Evan checked his watch, a mischievous grin spreading across his face. "Now? We catch the next flight to Egypt."

Chapter 11

Evan's boots scraped against the gravelly canyon floor, echoing eerily between the towering rock walls. He scanned the narrow passage ahead, senses primed for any sign of the mercenaries on their trail. Beside him, Sarah moved with cat-like tread, her dark eyes darting to every shadow.

"I don't like this," she murmured. "Too many places for an ambush."

Evan nodded, and the back of his neck prickled with unease. Silently, they pushed on, the winding canyon enveloping them in its stony grip.

Rounding a bend, Sarah froze. Evan nearly collided with her. Ahead, the canyon fell into a ravine, too wide to jump. Their path ended abruptly at its crumbling edge.

Sarah pointed. "Look, a fallen tree."

A long, skeletal trunk lay across the gap, a precarious bridge over the abyss. Evan hesitated. The tree didn't look nearly sturdy enough for them to cross.

"I don't know..." he began.

"No other way," Sarah said tersely. "Unless you've got wings hidden under that shirt."

Evan grimaced. She was right. They had no choice.

Carefully, they edged onto the makeshift bridge, their boots finding slippery purchase on the mossy bark. Don't look down, Evan told himself, eyes fixed ahead. The canyon yawned beneath them. His heart slammed against his ribs. Sweat beaded his brow despite the chill.

Nearly there. His breath escaped in a relieved gust--

A resounding crack split the air.

Evan's blood turned to ice. The tree trunk shuddered under their feet, and with a groan of twisting wood, it began to give way.

"Run!" Evan yelled.

He and Sarah sprinted the last few feet as the log collapsed into the ravine behind them. They threw themselves onto solid ground, chests heaving. Evan's pulse roared in his ears. That had been too close.

"We need to keep moving," Sarah said, scrambling up. "They probably heard that."

Evan rose on shaky legs. She was right. Their pursuers could be on them any second.

They hurried onward, the terrain growing steeper. Loose rocks slid treacherously underfoot. Evan's muscles burned as they climbed but didn't dare slow down. Not with the threat of the mercenaries behind them.

At last, they crested the ridge. Evan bent double, hands braced on his knees as he fought for breath. Sweat dripped into his eyes, blurring his vision.

He stiffened at the sound of approaching footsteps. Sarah yanked him down behind a jumble of boulders. They huddled there, hearts hammering, as booted feet marched past their hiding place.

Evan hardly dared breathe. The canyon amplified every scuff of leather on stone. He prayed the mercenaries wouldn't spot them.

After an agonizing wait, the footsteps faded into the distance. Evan finally released his held breath in a shaky exhale. That had been too close.

"We can't stay here," Sarah whispered. "Let's go."

On high alert, they slipped from their hiding place. The mercenaries' presence meant they were on the right track. Evan just hoped they could evade them long enough to achieve their goal. The secrets hidden here were too valuable to lose.

With cautious haste, they pressed onward. Their lives depended on it.

Sarah gestured wordlessly to a crumbling structure just ahead. It was little more than a tumble of weathered stones but offered some cover from unfriendly eyes.

They hurried over and ducked behind one of the remaining walls. Evan peered around cautiously. There was no sign of the mercenaries yet, but they couldn't be far behind.

"We need to keep moving," he murmured.

Sarah nodded in agreement. She jerked her chin toward an opening in the ruined wall. "There. Let's see where it goes."

They slipped through the gap into the darkness beyond with no better options. Evan blinked, eyes struggling to adjust after the bright desert sun. Slowly, the room took shape around them.

It was small and empty, save for a few pieces of broken pottery. At the back, an arched doorway led into another chamber. Evan and Sarah exchanged glances and moved toward it. Their footsteps echoed eerily in the enclosed space.

The next room was more significant, with intricate carvings lining the walls. Sarah reverently ran her fingers over them. "This place must be thousands of years old."

"Keep your guard up," Evan reminded her softly. These ruins still held secrets...and dangers.

He noticed an indentation in the wall at the back of the chamber. Brushing away cobwebs, he revealed a hidden lever. Heart racing, he pulled it.

With a grinding of ancient mechanisms, part of the wall slid away, revealing a dark tunnel that sloped down into the earth. Sarah gave a delighted laugh.

"A secret passage!" She lifted her torch, casting a flickering light down the tunnel. "Shall we see where it leads?"

Evan met her eager gaze. Discovery awaited below. He just hoped they could evade the mercenaries long enough to find it.

"Let's go."

Sarah took the lead as they descended into the tunnel, the flame from her torch causing shadows to dance ominously along the walls. The air grew more relaxed and damper, and soon, they could hear the faint sound of dripping water somewhere ahead.

Evan stayed close behind her, one hand trailing along the rough stone to keep his bearings in the darkness. He couldn't shake the uneasy feeling that they were being watched, though he saw no signs of pursuit yet.

After several twists and turns, the passage opened into a large chamber. Sarah lifted her torch higher, illuminating rows of stone pillars supporting a vaulted ceiling.

"Incredible," she breathed. "It looks like some kind of temple."

Evan nodded, eyes scanning the room. This seemed a likely place if there were clues about the artifact they sought.

They moved slowly between the pillars, the light glinting off veins of crystal in the rock walls. The only sound was the echo of their careful footsteps.

Then, from somewhere ahead came voices.

Evan and Sarah froze, exchanging an alarmed glance. The mercenaries! How had they discovered this place so quickly?

Heart pounding, Evan scanned the chamber. In the flickering torchlight, he spotted a small, dark alcove between two nearby pillars. He grabbed Sarah's arm and pulled her into it, pressing back against the stone as the voices drew steadily nearer.

They held their breath, praying the shadows would keep them hidden. The mercenaries' harsh voices were clear now, echoing through the temple as they searched it.

"No sign of 'em here either."

"They gotta be somewhere below. Keep looking."

The voices moved away again. Evan let out a quiet sigh of relief, then looked at Sarah. That had been too close. They couldn't let the mercenaries beat them to the artifact.

"Come on," he whispered. "We need to keep moving."

Sarah nodded, a determined look on her face. They slipped from their hiding place and moved as quietly as possible into the temple.

The voices faded into the distance, but they knew the mercenaries could return at any moment. Sarah's eyes continuously scanned the shadows, alert for the slightest sign of movement.

They reached a large central chamber, empty except for a raised stone altar. Torches flickered in sconces along the walls.

"This must have been where they performed rituals," Evan murmured. He moved closer to examine the altar. Sarah kept watch near the entrance, her muscles tensed.

Evan's fingers traced grooves carved into the stone surface. There seemed to be a pattern, but he couldn't make it out in the uncertain light. If he could just—

Sudden shouts echoed through the temple, far too close. The mercenaries had circled back!

Exchanging an alarmed glance with Sarah, Evan backed quickly away from the altar. They had seconds to find a hiding spot before—

Armed men stormed into the chamber, sweeping it with their flashlight beams. Evan and Sarah pressed into the shadows behind a pillar, praying the mercenaries' eyes would pass over them.

But the lights paused, focused on their hiding spot. They'd been seen!

Evan met Sarah's eyes. There is no choice now but to run for it.

Sarah reacted first, grabbing Evan's arm and sprinting toward the back of the chamber. Gunshots rang out, bullets ricocheting off the stone walls around them. Adrenaline pumped through Evan's veins as they ran, the altar and mercenaries blurring past.

Just ahead, he spotted a dark opening in the temple wall - some side passage. They dove through it, the gunshots echoing behind them.

The passage sloped downward at a steep angle. Evan struggled to keep his footing on the uneven stone steps. Sarah's hand on his arm steadied him.

"Do you think we lost them?" he whispered between ragged breaths.

"For now," Sarah replied tersely. "But we need to keep moving."

They continued downward, the air growing colder and damper. The light from Sarah's flashlight revealed mildew clinging to the walls and puddles on the steps.

After what felt like an eternity, the passage leveled out. They emerged into a massive underground chamber, its farthest reaches lost in darkness. Strange rock formations jutted up from the floor like alien sculptures.

Evan swept his light around, awed. "This place is incredible. It must extend under the whole temple complex."

"And the perfect place to get lost or trapped," Sarah said grimly. She drew her gun, eyes scanning the shadows for any sign of the mercenaries.

Evan moved carefully among the rock formations, looking for clues to the chamber's purpose. Carvings decorated some of the larger rocks, but he couldn't decipher them.

"Over here," Sarah called softly. She stood before a dark, yawning opening in the chamber wall. "Looks like another way out. We need to keep moving before they find us."

Evan nodded, taking one last glance around the ancient space. What other secrets might it hold? With a sigh, he turned to follow Sarah into the unknown.

Sarah led the way into the dark passage, her flashlight cutting a narrow beam through the inky blackness. The air was damp and heavy, smelling of ancient decay.

They moved as quickly and quietly as they could over the uneven ground. The winding passage sloped steadily upwards, leaving the underground chamber behind.

After what felt like hours, Sarah slowed. "I think I see the light up ahead," she whispered.

Moving cautiously, they crept forward until the passage opened into the blinding sunlight. Shielding their eyes, they stepped out onto a ledge overlooking a deep ravine. The lush jungle canopy swayed gently in the valley below.

"We made it out," Evan said with relief.

Sarah nodded, squinting against the glare. "Looks like we've got a good lead on them now. But we need to keep moving."

They followed the ledge until it connected with a narrow path snaking up the ravine wall. Then, they scrambled higher towards the jungle above, using exposed roots and loose rocks for handholds.

As the adrenaline of their escape wore off, Evan felt the aches in his muscles. But the sun on his face and fresh air revived him. He was amazed they'd made it this far.

Reaching the top, they pushed into the thick foliage. Moving swiftly but cautiously, they picked their way through the tangle of undergrowth. The sounds of birds and insects filled the air.

"Stay sharp," Sarah reminded softly. "We may have escaped the temple but are not out of danger yet."

Evan nodded, senses heightened for any sign they were still being pursued. For now, the jungle appeared untouched. But they couldn't let their guard down. The treasure - and answers - they sought were still ahead.

Sarah froze suddenly, grabbing Evan's arm. He followed her gaze to a smoke rising through the trees ahead.

"Campfire," she whispered. "We need to go around."

They moved slowly, scanning their surroundings. The jungle here was denser, the path narrow. One misstep could alert anyone nearby.

Evan's heart pounded as they neared the source of the smoke. He could hear voices now, speaking a language he didn't recognize—hunters, perhaps, or smugglers. Either way, they were not someone they wanted to encounter.

Sarah gestured to a thicket of bushes offering cover. They ducked behind it just as two men emerged from the trees, dressed in camouflage and carrying rifles.

Evan held his breath, willing them to pass quickly. But then a gunshot rang out in the distance.

The men froze, peering into the jungle. One shouted something to the other, and then they took off running.

Evan and Sarah exchanged worried glances. The gunshot likely meant their pursuers were closing in, so they had to keep moving.

Once the men were out of sight, Sarah and Evan slipped from their hiding spot and continued. The terrain grew steeper, but they pushed on, using vines and branches to pull themselves up.

Evan's muscles burned with effort, but determination drove him forward. He had to find the truth in these jungles, no matter the cost.

The gunshots grew louder now, spurring them higher. They were running out of time, but Evan knew they would face whatever lay ahead together.

Chapter 12

The flickering torchlight cast ominous shadows across the stone walls. Evan's eyes darted around the underground chamber, assessing the situation. Seven figures in dark robes surrounded them, faces obscured by hoods.

"The amulet," one demanded, his voice like gravel. "Hand it over."

Evan's grip tightened on his leather pouch. Inside was the golden amulet they had unearthed, an ancient relic of immense power. He exchanged a tense look with Sarah, whose jaw was clenched, and her eyes narrowed.

Like hell, we're handing it over. Evan's gaze flicked to a narrow opening in the wall behind the cloaked men. A way out.

He tilted his head subtly towards the passageway, hoping Sarah understood. Her eyes widened briefly before her expression hardened with resolve. She was ready.

With a burst of speed, Evan lunged for the opening, Sarah on his heels. The robed men shouted in surprise, scrambling after them. Evan's shoes pounded the stone floor, his satchel bouncing against his hip. He must get away! Protect the amulet!

He squeezed into the passageway, Sarah right behind him. It was a tight fit. Rough stone scraped Evan's shoulders as he shuffled sideways as fast as possible. Gloved hands grasped at them from behind. So close! Just a little further...

The passage opened into a small chamber. Evan and Sarah spilled out, spinning around. The robed men shoved into the narrow space, wedged together as they reached for their prey.

Evan's heart hammered. I was trapped again. But he'd be damned if he let these goons get the amulet.

"Get back!" Sarah yelled. With a mighty kick, she struck the wall above the passageway. Stone crumbled, sealing the opening. Dust filled the air.

They were safe, for now. Evan let out a shaky breath, adrenaline still surging through his veins.

"Let's find that exit," Sarah said. "Before they dig their way through."

Evan nodded. The amulet was secure in his bag, and Sarah was watching his back. Together, they would unravel the secrets of this ancient treasure.

Sarah swept her flashlight around the small chamber, the beam cutting through the dust and darkness. The stone walls were bare, with no visible exits.

"There's got to be a way out of here," Evan muttered, running his hands along the walls, searching for cracks or hidden switches.

Footsteps and angry shouts echoed from the other side of the blocked passageway. Their pursuers were already working to break through, and time was running out.

Evan's pulse quickened as his search yielded nothing. He turned to Sarah, who was examining the far wall, brow furrowed in concentration.

"Any luck?" he asked.

"Maybe..." Sarah trailed off, pressing on one of the stones. It shifted slightly under her touch. "Help me with this."

Together, they pushed on the stone. With the grinding of an ancient mechanism, a wall section swung inward. A rush of stale air hit their faces as the doorway opened into a small, dark chamber beyond.

Exchanging a determined glance, Evan and Sarah hurried through, the sounds of their enemies growing louder behind them. This had to lead somewhere. It just had to.

The beam of Sarah's flashlight revealed steep stone steps leading down into inky blackness. Their path forward was clear. They descended into the ancient darkness with the amulet heavy in Evan's satchel.

Sarah swept her flashlight beam over the crumbling stone steps as they descended further into the earth. The air grew colder and damper with each step, and their footsteps echoed eerily in the enclosed space.

"Where do you think this leads?" Sarah whispered.

"Hopefully, somewhere they won't find us," Evan replied, glancing back up the stairs. The angry shouts of their pursuers were growing fainter, but he knew it was only a matter of time before they discovered the hidden passageway.

After an eternity, the steps ended at an arched wooden door banded with black iron. Sarah ran her hand over the rough wood, fearing any traps or triggers.

"Only one way to find out," Evan said. Taking a deep breath, he pushed the door open.

Beyond was a large chamber shrouded in shadow. As Sarah's light played over the room, intricate hieroglyphs emerged from the darkness, painted on every surface. At the chamber's center sat a massive stone sarcophagus.

"It's a tomb," Sarah breathed. Moving closer, her light revealed a familiar name inscribed in the ancient language. "This is Pharaoh Seti's burial chamber. We found it!"

Evan hurried to the casket, hope rising within him. If the legends were true, the treasure they sought could finally be within reach. But his excitement turned to dread as he studied the cryptic hieroglyphs adorning the casket.

"Sarah, look at this," he said grimly. "It's a curse."

Sarah moved closer to examine the hieroglyphs Evan was pointing at. Though ancient Egyptian was not her most vital language skill, she could make out words like "death," "eternal," and "punishment." A chill went down her spine.

"Looks like trouble," she muttered. "Any ideas?"

Evan ran a hand through his hair in frustration. "I was afraid of this. Opening a pharaoh's tomb risks triggering an ancient curse. We have to figure out how to lift it before proceeding."

He began examining the rest of the casket, looking for clues. Sarah did the same, shining her light at the surrounding walls and floor. Strange symbols and geometric patterns covered every surface. There had to be something here to help them.

A scraping sound at the chamber entrance made them both freeze. The angry shouts were back, echoing down the passageway.

"They found the stairs," Evan said. "We're out of time."

Sarah's mind raced. If they couldn't break the curse quickly, they were doomed. Either their pursuers would capture them, or the curse would destroy them if they opened the coffin. They had to find an answer before it was too late.

"Over here," she whispered, beckoning Evan to the far wall. "I think this is something."

Evan rushed over to Sarah's examination of the far wall. In the beam of her flashlight, he could see a carved image of the jackal-headed god Anubis holding a set of scales with hieroglyphic text alongside it.

"It's a judgment scene," he murmured. "When a pharaoh died, Anubis would weigh their heart against a feather to judge their worthiness for the afterlife."

Footsteps echoed from the passageway leading into the chamber. Their pursuers were close.

"So we have to prove we're worthy to proceed," Sarah said. "But how?"

Evan's gaze fell on the scales carved into the wall. They looked removable, so he pried at the carving without hesitating until one scale came free in his hand.

"We each take a scale," he said. "They represent the weighing of our hearts and minds against chaos and order."

Sarah took the other scale. Just then, two men burst into the chamber, guns drawn.

"Hands up!" one shouted. "Step away from the sarcophagus!"

Evan and Sarah backed up, scales held high. The men advanced but slowed as they saw the scales.

"Chaos and order are balanced," Evan declared. "We have been judged worthy."

A rumbling sound filled the chamber. The men stumbled back in fear as part of the wall slid open beside the coffin.

Evan grasped Sarah's hand. "Now!"

They sprinted into the dark passageway as bullets ricocheted around them. But the judgment was complete. They had proven themselves and escaped.

The passageway was narrow and winding, forcing Evan and Sarah to flee in single file. Evan took the lead, one hand against the rough stone wall to guide himself in the darkness. Behind him, he could hear Sarah's hurried footsteps and panicked breathing.

"Just keep moving," he said over his shoulder. "We have to get as much distance between us and them as possible."

Sarah didn't respond, too focused on keeping up with Evan's swift pace. The footsteps and shouts of their pursuers echoed through the passageway, spurring them to move faster despite their exhaustion.

Suddenly, Evan slammed into a stone wall, causing Sarah to collide with his back. It was a dead end. Evan's hands desperately searched the dark for some latch or lever but found nothing. They were trapped.

Sarah pressed herself against the wall, eyes wide with fear. The glow of flashlights danced along the passage walls as the men drew nearer.

"What do we do?" Sarah whispered.

Evan's mind raced. Then, his gaze lifted to the ceiling. A ventilation shaft was set into the stone, just big enough for them to crawl through. Hope swelled in his chest.

"Up there," he said. "Help me get it open."

They strained to slide the grating free. As soon as the way was clear, Evan hoisted Sarah into the shaft. She reached down to pull him up just as their pursuers rounded the corner.

Gunshots erupted, but Evan and Sarah were crawling as fast as they could through the dusty shaft. They had escaped the maze of tunnels and lived to keep searching for another day.

Without hesitation, Evan and Sarah leap into the cool night air. Time seems to slow as the wind rushes past their ears. The city lights below blur into streaks of color. For a brief, terrifying moment, they are weightless.

Sarah squeezes her eyes shut, unable to watch the ground rush to meet them. Evan's arms flail as he tries to maneuver their bodies toward the roof's edge.

Impact. They hit the gravel hard, tucked into rolls to distribute the force. On landing, the wind knocked the wind from their lungs. For a long moment, they lay gasping, adrenaline coursing through their veins.

Evan recovers first, scrambling to his feet. He pulls Sarah up and gives her a quick once-over to check for injuries. Other than scrapes and bruises, they seem intact.

"Let's go," he urges. There's no time to waste.

Sarah gives a quick nod, regaining her bearings. She follows Evan's heels as they flee into the night, leaving their confused pursuers far behind. They stick to the shadows, disappearing like ghosts into the dark city.

Somehow, against all odds, they've made it. But new dangers await them on the path ahead. For now, they focus only on putting one foot in front of the other. Onward through the darkness, propelled by determination and a shared purpose that no one can extinguish.

Evan's mind races as they hurry through the dark streets. Where can they go so that their enemies won't find them? They need time to recover and to think, but every moment out in the open is a risk.

He glances back at Sarah, taking in her haggard appearance. They both look like they've been through a war zone. Her face is smeared with dirt, and her hair is coming loose from its ponytail. But her eyes are alert, scanning their surroundings for threats.

Evan makes a decision. "This way," he says, leading them down an alley. It's a risk, but less exposed than the main roads. They need somewhere to lay low for a few hours.

Sarah follows without question. She trusts Evan, even if his plans are often reckless. But they've kept each other alive this long.

The alley opens to a rundown parking lot behind an old apartment building. Evan heads straight for the metal fire escape, gesturing for Sarah to follow. They climb swiftly, feet echoing on the metal steps.

On the third floor, Evan jimmies open a window and helps Sarah inside. The apartment is empty, likely abandoned, and a thick layer of dust coats every surface.

"We should be safe here for now," Evan says, securing the window behind them.

Sarah sinks onto a moth-eaten couch, adrenaline seeping from her muscles. She aches all over, but the treasure—their life's work—is still safe. They will keep fighting, whatever it takes.

Evan sits beside her, neither speaking for a long moment. So much has happened in such a short period. But they cannot stop now.

"What's our next move?" Sarah finally asks, breaking the silence. She looks to Evan, knowing he will have a plan—he always does.

Evan takes a breath, mind turning over possibilities. "First, we rest. Then we finish this."

Sarah nods. Together, they will find a way.

Chapter 13

Evan squinted in the dim candlelight, leaning in close as Sarah's finger traced along the ancient papyrus. Hieroglyphs and cryptic symbols swirled before his eyes in an indecipherable code.

"Evan, look!" Sarah exclaimed, her voice echoing off the stone walls. "This symbol here, it's the same one we found on the sarcophagus in the tomb last week."

Evan's pulse quickened, possibilities racing through his mind. "You're right," he murmured. "That changes everything." His analytical brain kicked into overdrive, connecting dots and searching for patterns. Each new revelation brought them closer to unraveling the pharaoh's secrets.

Sarah's dark eyes shone with excitement. "If we can decode this text, it may lead us to his hidden treasure chamber," she said rapidly and enthusiastically. "This could be the breakthrough we've been searching for!"

"Let's not get ahead of ourselves," Evan cautioned, but he couldn't deny the anticipation building within him. This ancient language frustrated yet enthralled him. He itched to transcribe the symbols and translate their meaning.

Sarah nodded, her smile fading. "You're right; we need to be careful." Her voice dropped to a whisper. "We don't know who else might be after this treasure." Her eyes darted around the shadowy chamber.

Evan felt the familiar thrill of discovery tempered by hard-won caution. With Sarah, he would unravel this mystery, no matter the danger. The answers were here, locked in these cryptic codes. All they needed was the key.

Sarah bent over the table and furrowed her brow as she examined the ancient texts. Her finger traced along the intricate hieroglyphs, following the flow of symbols across cracked papyrus.

"Here," she murmured, tapping a section on the scroll. "This part references 'the chamber of the great ruler, hidden from mortal eyes.'"

Evan's pulse quickened. He grabbed his notebook and hastily scribbled down the symbols and their translations. Each revelation brought them closer to uncovering secrets lost for millennia.

"If we can break the code, we may find a map to the hidden tomb," he said. "Who knows what treasures could be concealed there?"

Sarah nodded, her expression guarded. "Yes, but we must be discreet. This knowledge is dangerous in the wrong hands."

Evan understood her caution. Throughout his career, he had seen artifacts pillaged and sites desecrated by those seeking personal gain. He would not let that happen here.

The thrill of discovery warred with prudence. This ancient language frustrated yet enthralled him. He yearned to decipher its secrets and reveal its hidden meanings.

With Sarah at his side, he would unravel the mystery entombed in these ancient texts. The answers were here, locked in cryptic symbols and obscured references. Together, they would find the key.

Sarah traced her finger along the cracked papyrus, following a winding path of intricate symbols. Her brow furrowed in concentration as she studied the ancient text.

"Here," she said, tapping a section. "This references 'the chamber hidden beneath the carved eye.'"

Evan's pulse quickened. He scribbled notes feverishly, translating the glyphs. Each revelation brought them closer to uncovering secrets lost for eons.

"If we decode this map, it could lead us to the pharaoh's tomb," he said. "Imagine what knowledge has been buried there all these centuries."

Sarah nodded, her expression guarded. "Yes, but we must keep this discovery quiet. This knowledge in the wrong hands..." She trailed off, her implication clear.

Evan understood her caution. He had seen artifacts pillaged and sites desecrated by those seeking personal gain. That would not happen here. Not on his watch.

His thirst for knowledge warred with prudence. This cryptic language enthralled yet frustrated him. He yearned to unravel its mysteries and reveal its concealed truths.

With Sarah beside him, he would decipher the riddle entombed in these ancient texts. The answers were here, obscured in arcane symbols and veiled references. Together, they would find the key that unlocked the door to antiquity's secrets.

Sarah's eyes met Evan's, a silent understanding passing between them. This discovery needed to remain hidden, shared only between them.

Evan gathered up the fragile papyri, carefully rolling and securing them. Sarah double-checked her backpack, taking stock of provisions for their impending journey into the desert.

She slipped an extra canteen of water into the bag and grabbed a wide-brimmed hat to shield her fair skin from the harsh sun. Her worn but sturdy boots were ready to carry her over rough terrain.

Evan finished organizing his equipment, ensuring his journal and tools were secure. This would be a long trek through treacherous conditions, and they both understood the risks, but the potential rewards were too great to ignore.

Sarah pulled a crumpled map from her pocket, tracing the route with her finger.

"Once we leave the valley, there will be no settlements for two hundred miles," she said. Evan nodded, his jaw set with determination.

"We'll take it slow and conserve our resources. But I know we can make it," he replied.

Sarah smiled, her green eyes glinting. "Well then, what are we waiting for? Let's go uncover some history."

She slung her backpack over her shoulders and headed for the door, Evan following close behind. This would be the adventure of a lifetime, revealing secrets hidden for millennia. Together, they would illuminate the past.

The sun beat down relentlessly as Evan and Sarah trekked across the vast expanse of desert. The landscape stretched as far as the eye could see, an endless sea of dunes and rocky outcroppings.

Evan paused to take a swig from his canteen, the tepid water offering little relief from the oppressive heat. Rivulets of sweat dripped down his back as he forged ahead. Beside him, Sarah shielded her eyes against the harsh glare, scanning the horizon for landmarks to guide them.

The map crinkled in Evan's pocket, their path marked in faded pencil. Each mile brought them closer to the hidden oasis, but the distance was deceptive in the desert. What looked manageable on paper became an ordeal under the baking sun.

As the day wore on, the straps of their packs dug into shoulders unaccustomed to such loads. Their pace slowed, but they pressed forward, step after arduous step. Stopping to rest brought little comfort as the sand burned through their clothes.

A chill crept through the night air when the sun finally dipped below the dunes. Evan gathered brush and lit a small fire, the flickering light keeping the darkness at bay. With weary limbs, he unfurled his bedroll beside Sarah's. Tomorrow, they would rise and continue their quest. There could be no turning back now.

Evan glanced at his companion as she gazed thoughtfully into the flames. "Do you think we'll find it?" he asked quietly.

Sarah's eyes shone with resolve. "I know we will," she said firmly. Evan smiled and closed his eyes, comforted by her confidence. Together, they would uncover the secrets of the past.

The sun crested over the dunes, bathing the desert in a warm golden glow. Evan shielded his eyes as he scanned the horizon, searching for their destination. A patch of vibrant green was nestled between two towering cliffs.

"The oasis!" Evan exclaimed. Adrenaline flooded his veins. After days of endless sand, they had finally arrived.

Sarah scrambled up the dune beside him, catching her breath as she took the sight. "We made it," she breathed.

They approached cautiously on foot, alert for any sign of danger. But the oasis appeared untouched, a sanctuary untouched by time. Palm trees swayed gently in the morning breeze, and birds sang overhead. The azure pool in the center was still and serene.

Kneeling at the water's edge, Evan filled his canteen and splashed his face. The cool liquid soothed his parched skin. This place felt sacred, imbued with an ancient power.

Sarah's fingers traced the weathered carvings adorning the rocky overhang. "Look at the craftsmanship," she murmured. "This oasis could have sustained generations."

Evan nodded, eyes scanning their surroundings. He could almost see ghosts of the past moving among the trees. What secrets lay buried here? His curiosity burned.

"Let's take a look around," he suggested. Their journey was not over yet. Together, they delved deeper into the oasis, drawn by the promise of discovery.

Sarah's eyes widened as they entered a clearing at the heart of the oasis. Carved into the cliff face was an elaborate stone doorway flanked by statues of jackal-headed gods.

"A hidden temple," she breathed. "Just like the map indicated."

Evan ran his hand over the intricate hieroglyphs surrounding the entrance. "These carvings tell the story of the treasure within. We're close now," he said.

They stepped across the threshold with bated breath into the cool, dark interior. Flickering torchlight cast dancing shadows across the painted walls, and the stale air was heavy with mystery.

Evan's senses were on high alert, scanning for any signs of traps or tricks. But the temple appeared untouched, frozen in time. Their soft footsteps echoed eerily as they ventured deeper inside.

Sarah gasped as she rounded a corner. Before them lay a vast chamber, pillars carved with celestial symbols soaring overhead. At the far end sat an ornate stone altar.

"This is it," Evan whispered, his pulse racing. Together, they cautiously crossed the chamber. This was hallowed ground, imbued with ancient power. What secrets had lain hidden for centuries, awaiting their arrival?

As one, they turned to face the altar, a thrill of anticipation running through them. The treasure was close, waiting to be unearthed.

Sarah reached towards the altar, hands trembling. This was the moment they had been waiting for, the culmination of their research and perseverance. Her fingers brushed the excellent stone surface, tracing the intricate carvings.

Suddenly, a sharp voice cut through the stillness.

"Stop right there!" it barked. "Step away from the altar!"

Sarah jerked her hand back as though burned. Beside her, Evan tensed, eyes darting around the shadowy chamber. Out of the gloom emerged half a dozen figures, faces obscured by dark masks. Evan's heart sank. It was the ruthless organization they had hoped to avoid.

The apparent leader stepped forward, coarse laughter echoing around the temple walls.

"Did you think you could just waltz here and take the treasure?" he sneered. Behind him, his cronies snickered. "Hand it over, nice and easy now."

Evan glanced at Sarah, seeing his defiance mirrored in her eyes. After everything they had endured, they would not back down without a fight. The treasure belonged in a museum, not lining these thieves' pockets.

"We can't let you take it," Evan said firmly, standing before the altar. "This discovery belongs to all humanity. We won't let you misuse it."

The leader's eyes narrowed dangerously. "Looks like we'll have to take it by force then," he growled, drawing a wicked curved blade. "But don't say I didn't warn you..."

Evan and Sarah braced themselves, united in purpose. Come what may, they would protect the secrets of this ancient temple!

The leader lunged forward, his blade glinting in the torchlight. Evan dove sideways, the knife barely missing him. Sarah grabbed a heavy artifact off the altar and hurled it at their attackers. The stone caught one person square in the face, and he went down with a shout.

"Grab the codex!" Evan yelled, grappling with another thief. Sarah snatched up the ancient book, dodging a blow from behind. She slammed the codex into her assailant's head, and he crumpled.

Evan traded punches with the brute, trying to wrestle him down. He kneed the man in the stomach and shoved him back. Out of his eye, he saw the leader sneaking up behind Sarah.

"Look out!" Evan shouted. Too late. The leader seized Sarah's arm, twisting violently. She cried out in pain, codex tumbling from her grasp.

Rage coursed through Evan's veins. He tackled the leader with all his strength, both men crashing to the hard stone floor. They exchanged blows, Evan's glasses cracking. He hardly noticed, consumed by fury. With a final punch, the leader went limp.

Evan scrambled to Sarah's side, checking her injured arm. "Can you move it?" he asked worriedly. She winced but nodded.

"We have to go now!" Grabbing the codex, they fled the chamber and sprinted into the night, leaving the ransacked temple and defeated thieves behind. Their desperate fight was over, but new perils awaited them outside. Gritting their teeth against the pain, Evan and Sarah carried on. The treasure was safe - for the moment.

Evan and Sarah ran through the moonlit desert, adrenaline pumping through their veins. The night air was cold against their sweat-slicked skin. Evan's hand throbbed where he had slugged the thief leader. He was sure some fingers were broken, but there was no time to stop and tend wounds.

Sarah cradled the ancient codex to her chest with her good arm. It was the treasure that had nearly cost them their lives. Was it worth this pain and bloodshed? Evan wasn't sure, but he knew they could not let such knowledge fall into the hands of those who would abuse its power.

As the dark silhouette of the temple disappeared behind a dune, Evan risked a glance over his shoulder. No sign of pursuit. Yet. He caught Sarah's eye, and she gave a curt nod. Keep going.

They had been in dire straits before, but something about this felt different. The codex was no ordinary find. Whatever secrets it contained had dangerous men willing to kill for them. Evan and Sarah had to decipher its mysteries before anyone else. The future might depend on it.

As the adrenaline ebbed, the bite of the cold night sank into Evan's bones. His injuries throbbed in time with his rapid heartbeat. He focused on putting one foot in front of the other across the shifting sands.

Beside him, Sarah's breath came in pained gasps. She was struggling, too, but her dark eyes remained hard with determination. She would not give up, and neither would he.

By the time the lights of Cairo appeared on the horizon, both were nearly spent. Yet at the sight of that familiar skyline, Evan felt hope swell within him. They had made it. Beat the odds once again. And with the codex's secrets now in their possession, a new chapter of discovery was about to unfold.

Chapter 14

The flickering torchlight cast ominous shadows across the stone walls of the underground chamber. Evan's eyes darted around, taking in the half dozen black-clad figures surrounding them. Their faces were obscured by dark masks, except for cold, merciless eyes.

"The treasure," one demanded, his voice muffled. "Hand it over."

Evan shifted closer to Sarah, his mind racing. His gaze fell upon a narrow opening in the chamber's far wall. A possible escape route. He caught Sarah's eye and tilted his head almost imperceptibly toward the passage. She gave a tiny nod.

In a blur of movement, they sprinted for the opening. Shouts of surprise erupted behind them as their pursuers gave chase. Evan's lungs burned as he plunged into near-darkness, Sarah's footsteps echoing his own. Up ahead, he could make out a widening in the passage.

They burst into an enormous cavern, ancient statues and artifacts scattered about. Staying low, they weaved between weathered pillars, using the maze-like layout to their advantage. Their pursuers' heavy footfalls reverberated through the chamber. Evan's pulse pounded as he and Sarah scrambled into the shadows. For now, they had slipped their enemy's grasp, but they weren't out of danger yet...

Sarah's breath came in ragged gasps as she pressed against the pillar. The angry shouts of her pursuers echoed around the cavern as they searched for her and Evan.

She risked a peek around the pillar, and her eyes widened. The cavern was filled with artifacts - statues, urns, tablets - a treasure trove from ancient civilizations. If they could escape, what knowledge might be gained from studying them?

But now was not the time for such thoughts. Evan caught her gaze from behind an adjacent pillar and gestured ahead. A giant statue of Anubis, the jackal-headed Egyptian god of the underworld, loomed in the shadows. Sarah nodded, and they moved silently toward it, using the statues for cover.

The shouts were getting closer. As they reached the Anubis statue, Sarah noticed a small indent at the base, barely visible in the gloom. She instinctively pressed it.

With a grinding of stone on stone, the statue shifted, and a dark opening appeared behind it—a hidden passage!

"This way," Sarah whispered urgently. She slipped through the opening, Evan close behind. The statue slid back just as their pursuers entered the cavern.

Safe for the moment, they hurried down the passage. Even as her feet flew over the rough ground, Sarah's mind raced. Each step took them closer to escape...or even deeper into danger.

Evan and Sarah raced down the narrow passageway, their flashlights casting dancing shadows on the ancient stone walls. The tunnel sloped steadily downward, bringing them even deeper into the earth.

They soon reached a fork, and Sarah hesitated. "Which way?"

Evan pointed left. "That one slopes upward. It might lead us out."

They only went a short distance when the unmistakable echo of pursuing footsteps reached them. The organization's members had discovered the hidden entrance!

Sarah swallowed hard, willing her feet faster. Just ahead, the passage opened into an enormous cavern. They emerged cautiously, sweeping their flashlights around.

Suddenly, bullets ricocheted off the stone pillars around them. Sarah dove behind a granite statue of Horus as Evan rolled into cover beside a casket.

"We're pinned down!" Evan shouted over the barrage.

Sarah's mind raced. They couldn't go back, and the cavern seemed to have no other exits. Then, she noticed a small lever protruding from the base of the Horus statue. An escape route. She leaned out, gunshots narrowly missing her, and yanked the lever.

With a rumble, the statue slid sideways, revealing a dark opening. "Evan, this way!" Sarah cried.

As their pursuers stormed into the cavern, they scrambled into the passageway, weapons raised. The stone door slid closed, sealing them in musty darkness.

They had eluded the organization again but knew the dangers ahead.

Sarah swept her flashlight beam over their new surroundings. The passageway was narrow, with rough stone walls and a low ceiling, and it seemed to stretch endlessly into the darkness.

"Any idea where this leads?" Evan whispered.

Sarah shook her head. "No telling. But forward is our only option now."

They moved cautiously, senses on high alert. The tunnel sloped gradually downward, taking them deeper into the ancient complex.

After several tense minutes, Sarah noticed the passage widening ahead. Her flashlight revealed a stone archway opening into a massive cavern. She stepped through and swept her light around in awe.

The cavern was enormous, with vaulted ceilings disappearing into blackness. Intricate pillars lined the edges, carved with hieroglyphs and images of pharaohs. At the far end, Sarah's light glinted off something. Water?

As they moved closer, the sound of rushing water reached their ears. To their dismay, it was a churning underground river, too wide to jump, its current violent. The only way across was a narrow stone ledge hugging the cavern wall.

Evan eyed the ledge dubiously. "Think it will hold us?"

Sarah bit her lip. "It's our only way forward."

She stepped gingerly onto the ledge, pressing herself flat against the wall. Inch by inch, she shuffled sideways, the ledge barely wide enough for her feet. Evan followed, neither daring to look down into the frothing water below.

They were halfway across when a barrage of gunshots exploded behind them. Sarah's heart leaped into her throat as bullets ricocheted off the stone walls. Their pursuers had caught up!

"Go, go!" Evan yelled. Sarah quickened her shuffle, the ledge beginning to crumble under their feet. Just a little farther...

With a final desperate leap, they cleared the ledge, collapsing in a heap on solid ground as the ledge gave way and plunging into the river below. There was no going back now. Onward through the ancient depths, ready or not.

Sarah's hands shook as she swept her flashlight around the new chamber. More tunnels branched off in all directions, disappearing into darkness. Which way now?

Evan pointed to the leftmost tunnel. "That one slopes upward. It might lead to the surface," he said.

They hurried into the passage, their footfalls echoing off the close walls. As they ascended, the air grew warmer and drier.

Rounding a corner, Sarah yelped as a barrage of darts shot from the wall. Evan yanked her back just in time. Squinting in the dim light, he made out holes lining the walls ahead.

"Booby traps," he muttered. "Watch your step."

Slowly, carefully, they picked their way down the corridor, Evan testing each step before putting his weight down. Twice more hidden traps were unleashed, but they managed to trigger them safely from a distance using rocks.

Finally, the passage opened into a large circular chamber. Intricate carvings and statues adorned the walls, and a massive stone slab sealed off the far side. Sunlight filtered through cracks in the ceiling.

"The exit must be just on the other side!" Evan said.

As she examined the stone slab, Sarah's eyes lit up, and she ran her hands over the carved symbols.

"It's just like the entrance," she murmured. "If I can decode the pattern..."

Shouts echoed from the tunnel behind them, accompanied by approaching footsteps, and their time had run out.

Sarah's fingers flew over the ancient carvings, deciphering the intricate code as Evan watched the tunnel opening. Her mind raced—she had to solve this quickly before their pursuers arrived.

The shouts grew louder. Evan picked up a rock, ready to stall them.

"I think I've got it!" Sarah said. She pressed a series of symbols in sequence. With a deep groan, the massive slab slid inward. Blinding sunlight flooded the chamber.

Evan squinted against the sudden brightness. "Let's go!"

They rushed through the opening, emerging onto a narrow rocky ledge high on the canyon wall. Evan closed the stone door behind them just as their pursuers reached the chamber.

Shielding their eyes, Evan and Sarah stumbled along the steep ledge. The canyon fell away hundreds of feet below them. They had to keep moving.

The ledge narrowed perilously before opening onto a small plateau. Checking behind them, Evan saw no sign of pursuit yet.

"We can't stop," he panted. "They'll be right behind us."

Sarah scanned the canyon. "There - a path leads down."

They hurried to the steep, zigzagging trail, hoping speed and terrain could finally shake their relentless hunters. As the plateau disappeared from view, Evan allowed himself a glimmer of hope. They might make it out alive.

Sarah led the way down the steep and treacherous path, loose rocks skittering under their feet. Evan followed close behind, glancing back periodically to check for any signs of pursuit. The narrow trail switchbacked sharply down the canyon wall. One misstep would send them plunging to their deaths.

About halfway down, the trail passed through a narrow cleft in the rock. Sarah slowed, feeling along the rock walls.

"There must be some kind of hidden door or passage," she said. "Many of these canyons have built-in escape routes."

Evan kept watch on the trail above them. "Hurry, they can't be far behind."

Sarah's fingers slid over a barely perceptible groove in the rock. Pressing it, a hidden door swung inward. They slipped inside just as shouts echoed from above.

The hidden passageway was pitch black. Sarah fished a small flashlight from her pack and flicked it on, illuminating rough stone walls on either side.

"Which way?" Evan whispered.

Sarah pointed the flashlight in both directions. The passage ended abruptly to the left after about ten feet, and to the right, it continued into darkness.

"Right it is," she said.

They moved as quickly and quietly as they could down the passage. It sloped gradually downward, twisting and turning. Their harsh breathing echoed off the closed walls.

After what seemed an eternity, Sarah's light glinted off something ahead. An ancient wooden door bound in tarnished bronze bands.

"This could be our way out," Evan said.

Sarah nodded. "Or into even more danger. We have to change it."

Taking a deep breath, she pushed open the door.

Chapter 15

The flickering torchlight cast dancing shadows across the ancient stone walls as Evan and Sarah descended the crumbling staircase. Evan's heart pounded against his ribs—after months of research and dead ends, they finally held the key to unlocking the hidden chamber's secrets.

Beside him, Sarah tensed, her dark eyes scanning the darkness. Evan knew she was replaying the ambushes and betrayals of her past, waiting for the trap to spring. But he squeezed her hand reassuringly. "We're so close," he whispered.

The stairs ended abruptly, opening into a vast underground chamber. Evan raised his torch, illuminating walls covered in intricate hieroglyphs and carvings. Sarah gasped, reaching out to trace an image of Anubis weighing a deceased's heart.

"It's just as the legends describe," Evan breathed. As they explored further, depictions emerged of a powerful pharaoh who hid his treasures to prevent tomb raiders from stealing them.

Sarah paused before a section showing warriors protecting the riches. "Looks like we weren't the first to go searching," she murmured.

Evan's eyes locked onto a pedestal at the chamber's center. "There," he said, starting toward it. "If the clues are right, that tablet is the final key."

Sarah grabbed his arm, pointing at the hieroglyphs near the pedestal. "Wait—look."

Together, they read the ancient warning: only those pure of heart could unlock the treasure's power. Greed would unleash catastrophe.

Evan met Sarah's gaze. "Are we doing the right thing?"

She considered, then squeezed his hand again. "As long as we stay true to ourselves."

Reassured, they continued, minds focused on uncovering history rather than material riches. When they reached the pedestal, Evan reverently lifted the tablet, hoping its secrets would illuminate the past.

Evan's examination of the tablet was interrupted by the sound of approaching footsteps echoing through the chamber. He quickly set the tablet back down and exchanged an anxious glance with Sarah. Moving swiftly, they darted behind a large pillar, pressing themselves into the shadows and holding their breath.

Moments later, several figures entered the chamber, the glow from their flashlights dancing along the walls. Evan recognized them as members of the Order, the ruthless organization pursuing the same ancient clues. Sarah tensed beside him; her eyes narrowed as the group spread out, shining their lights over the carvings and artifacts.

"Fan out and search the chamber," one of them barked. "The tablet must be here."

Evan gritted his teeth, exchanging a meaningful look with Sarah. Unlike Evan and Sarah, who wished to preserve history, they knew the Order sought the treasure for their gain.

One of the Order members approached the pedestal, his eyes gleaming with greed. "Here it is," he exclaimed, reaching for the tablet.

Evan had to fight the urge to leap out and stop him. Beside him, Sarah looked ready to pounce as well. They remained hidden, hoping the Order would take what they came for and leave.

But as the man lifted the tablet from the pedestal, an eerie glow emerged from within, bathing the chamber in an unearthly light. He stared at it in awe, realization dawning.

"This is no mere clue," he shouted. "We've found the key to unlocking the greatest power known to man!"

Evan and Sarah exchanged horrified looks. They had to act fast before the Order unleashed forces beyond their control.

With the Order members momentarily blinded by the tablet's glow, Evan seized the chance. He nodded to Sarah, and they swiftly but silently slipped from their hiding spot behind the pillar. Years of working together, they had honed their ability to communicate without words. Sarah's eyes said it all - hurry.

They crept along the chamber walls, ducking behind artifacts and sculptures. Evan's heart pounded, and the tablet's unearthly glow cast moving shadows that tricked his eyes. Still, he focused, putting one foot carefully in front of the other—just a little closer...

The Order leader reverently held the tablet, oblivious to Evan and Sarah's approach. "At last, the power is ours," he proclaimed. "With this, we can reshape the world as we see fit."

Evan's jaw clenched. He would not let them twist such knowledge to their ends. As he and Sarah reached the central dais, he steeled himself. The time he had come. He launched forward with lightning reflexes, wrenching the tablet from the leader's grasp.

"No!" the man cried, lunging to regain the relic. But Sarah was faster, sweeping his feet out from under him. He crashed to the ground as Evan and Sarah sprinted for the exit, the glowing tablet in hand. Shouts echoed behind them as the Order gave chase, but Evan and Sarah's head start gave them a fighting chance. They just had to make it outside, where their allies awaited. The ancient knowledge would be safe once more.

Sarah's breath came in sharp bursts as she sprinted down the twisting passageway beside Evan. She could hear the angry shouts of the Order members gaining on them from behind. Clutching the glowing tablet tight against her chest, she poured all her energy into her legs, willing them to go faster.

Just a little further. The exit can't be much farther. She repeated the words like a mantra, blocking out the stitch in her side and the trembling of exhausted muscles.

Beside her, Evan's face was set in determination, his eyes fixed ahead. She knew he would get them out of this. He had to.

As she rounded a corner, Sarah's heart leaped at the sight of sunlight streaming through an opening in the rock wall just ahead. Freedom!

With a final burst of speed, they cleared the passageway, bursting into the open air and momentary safety. Evan spun around, ready to seal the exit behind them.

But before he could act, a dark figure filled the opening, the light silhouetting him menacingly. It was the Order's leader.

"You can't stop us," he growled. "The power will be ours."

Evan stepped protectively in front of Sarah, shielding the tablet. She felt a swell of gratitude for her friend's bravery.

"Over my dead body," Evan spat back through gritted teeth.

The standoff stretched tense seconds...before an earth-shattering roar split the air. Sarah's eyes shot upwards in shock. A helicopter! Their backup had arrived!

As it hovered overhead, ropes dropped down, just as planned. Gripping Evan's arm, Sarah turned and ran for them. They scrambled up the ropes as bullets ricocheted off the rocks around them. But soon, they were rising up and away; the Order leader left shouting furiously below.

They had done it—together, just like always. Sarah met Evan's eyes, and they exchanged a grin. The adventure wasn't over yet.

Sarah's lungs burned as she sprinted through the ancient chamber, weaving between massive stone pillars to lose their pursuers. Evan was right on her heels, clutching the precious tablet tightly to his chest.

"We can't outrun them forever!" Evan shouted over the pounding footsteps echoing behind them.

Sarah desperately scanned the room, looking for anything that might help. Up ahead, she spotted a dark alcove partially concealed behind a statue.

"This way!" she yelled, grabbing Evan's arm and pulling him along.

They ducked into the alcove, pressing themselves flat against the wall and trying to control their ragged breathing. The footsteps grew louder as the Order members drew near.

Sarah exchanged a tense look with Evan. They both knew it would all be over if they were discovered now—the tablet, their research, their lives—all gone instantly.

As the footsteps reached the opening of the alcove, Sarah squeezed her eyes shut, bracing herself. This was it.

Suddenly, a loud rumbling sounded from deep within the chamber. Sarah's eyes flew open as the ground began to shake violently beneath them. She clutched at the wall to keep her balance.

"It's a trap!" Evan yelled over the noise. "An earthquake triggered!"

Sarah watched in awe as stone slabs slid away from the chamber floor, revealing a hidden pit. With cries of shock, the Order members tumbled into the inky blackness. The rumbling ceased as quickly as it had started, and an eerie silence fell over the chamber.

"Let's get out of here before the trap resets," Sarah said. They slipped out of the alcove and hurried on, the tablet's secret still safe.

Sarah's heart pounded as they raced through the twisting passages. She could still hear shouts and angry curses from the pit trap, so they knew the Order wasn't far behind.

Rounding a corner, Sarah skidded to a stop. A solid stone wall blocked their path, making it a dead end.

"No, no!" she cried in frustration, slamming her fist against the unyielding rock. This couldn't be how it ended. Not when they were so close.

She turned to see Evan studying the wall intently, his fingers tracing lightly over the carved hieroglyphs.

"These symbols," he murmured. "I've seen them before."

Sarah watched hopefully as understanding dawned on Evan's face.

"Of course!" he exclaimed. "The temple blueprints showed a hidden passage triggered by."

He pressed firmly on three glyphs in quick succession. With a deep groan, the wall slowly slid sideways, revealing a dark tunnel sloping downwards.

Sarah gasped. "Evan, you did it!"

Glancing back once at the sounds of pursuit, they plunged into the passageway. They moved as swiftly as they dared in the inky blackness and felt their way down the tunnel.

After what seemed an eternity, Sarah noticed a soft glow ahead. Rounding a final bend, the tunnel opened up into an immense cavern.

Sarah's jaw dropped. The cavern glimmered with a pale golden light reflecting off countless treasures—statues, coins, and jewelry, all perfectly preserved. It was a king's ransom from centuries ago, hidden from the world.

"Magnificent," Evan breathed. For a moment, they stood in awe, the danger momentarily forgotten.

Then Evan turned, resolve in his eyes. "We should go. This belongs to the past."

Sarah nodded reluctantly. Some secrets were not meant to be disturbed. With a last lingering look, they turned and hurried on, the cavern's treasures fading back into legend.

Sarah and Evan hurried through the glimmering cavern, the sounds of their pursuers growing louder behind them.

Sarah's eyes scanned the shadows, seeking an escape route. But the cavern seemed to have only one entrance - the way they had come.

"Evan," she whispered urgently. "We're trapped!"

He paused, thinking furiously. "There must be a way out. These ancients were ingenious."

Sarah shook her head in frustration. Then, her gaze fell on a stone tablet resting on a pedestal in the cavern's center. Intricate carvings and glyphs covered its surface.

"Could that be..." she murmured. Evan followed her gaze, eyes lighting up.

"The final clue!" He rushed to the tablet, gently lifting it from its resting place. "This is no mere clue - it's the key!"

Sarah joined him, peering closely at the markings. Understanding began to surface through the fog of adrenaline and fear.

"A key that unlocks...power," she said slowly. "Power that could be misused."

Heavy footsteps echoed down the passage behind them. Evan's hands clenched on the tablet.

"We can't let them have this," he said grimly. Meeting Sarah's eyes, he saw the exact resolution there.

With a mighty heave, they slammed the tablet to the cavern floor. With a resounding crack, it shattered into fragments.

A blinding flash lit the cavern, forcing them to shield their eyes. When they could see again, the cavern was empty but for glimmering treasure and broken stone.

Their pursuers had vanished. The secret - whatever it was - would remain hidden.

Sarah let out a shaky breath, leaning against the cavern wall. Evan ran a hand through his hair, glancing around warily as if expecting their foes to reappear.

"We did it," he said finally. "It's over."

Sarah nodded, though her posture remained tense. "For now. But we should move quickly before they find another way in."

With a last look around the glittering cavern, they turned toward the passage that had led them there. It was time to leave this place, hopefully for good.

The journey back was arduous. Adrenaline had faded, leaving bone-deep exhaustion in its wake. They had to pause frequently to rest and tend to their injuries from the day's trials.

Despite their weariness, an air of triumph buoyed their steps. The organization might remain a threat, but at least knowledge has prevailed over greed for today.

As they neared the surface, Evan glanced at his companion with a tired smile. "We make a good team, Dr. Johnson."

Sarah huffed a laugh. "That we do, Dr. Reynolds. But let's not do this again anytime soon."

Daylight streamed into the passage ahead. The adventure was over, but the bond forged between them would remain. Side by side, the two explorers stepped out into the sun, looking toward new horizons.

Sarah shielded her eyes against the harsh sunlight as they emerged from the tomb. Despite her exhaustion, she took a moment to breathe in the fresh desert air. After hours underground, even the arid climate felt like a blessing.

Beside her, Evan blinked rapidly, letting his vision adjust. His clothes were filthy and torn in places from their close call, but his eyes shone with exhilaration.

"Quite a trip, eh?" he said. "Worth all the scrapes and bruises."

Sarah shook her head with a wry smile. "You're unbelievable. We barely make it out alive, and you're ready to go again."

"Oh, come on, you have to admit it was thrilling," Evan said. "Discovering that hidden chamber, deciphering the clues...this is what we live for!"

His enthusiasm was infectious. As much as the danger had worried her, Sarah couldn't deny the allure of unraveling ancient secrets.

"Alright," she conceded. "It was pretty incredible. That tablet alone could rewrite history." A pang of regret pierced her at the memory of its destruction. But it had been necessary.

Evan's excitement dimmed at the thought. "I just hope we made the right call," he murmured.

Sarah grasped his shoulder firmly. "We did. That knowledge was in the wrong hands..." she trailed off with a shake. Let's focus on the positives. We learned much about this culture, even if we couldn't preserve the artifacts. That's still an invaluable contribution."

Evan nodded, determination returning to his eyes. "You're right. Our work matters, with or without physical treasures."

With a deep breath, he turned to gaze out at the desert. "So, what's next for the intrepid explorers?"

Sarah smiled and pulled out her map. "Well, there's a newly discovered temple complex not far from where I've been meaning to investigate..."

Evan laughed. "Lead the way, partner."

They set off again side by side. The future was promising, and neither could wait to unravel its mysteries.

Chapter 16

The aroma of freshly brewed coffee permeated the busy café as Evan and Sarah slipped into a corner booth. Exhaustion weighed on their shoulders after the harrowing events of the past few days.

Evan ran a hand through his messy hair. "That was too close for comfort back there. I thought we were done for when that ceiling started to collapse."

Sarah nodded, her eyes darting around the room as she took in every detail. "If I hadn't noticed that weak support beam, we'd be buried under a ton of rubble right now."

"We make quite the team, don't we?" Evan said. "Your sharp eye has gotten us out of more than one tight spot."

"And we never would have made it this far without your relentless pursuit of the truth," Sarah replied, a hint of a smile touching her lips. "I don't know anyone else who could decipher that cryptic code."

Evan sighed, the weight of their quest settling over him once more. "I just hope it leads us to the answers we seek. We're running out of time."

Sarah reached across the table and gently touched his arm. "We'll figure this out," she said. "We've come too far to give up now. Whatever challenges lie ahead, we'll face them together."

Evan met her steadfast gaze, drawing strength from her determination. He knew he could unravel even the most confounding mystery with Sarah by his side. The past held its secrets close, but he would uncover the truth, no matter the cost.

Sarah's words resonated with Evan. Here they were, two passionate academics united by a shared purpose - to uncover the mysteries of the past and reveal long-buried truths. Though their journey had been fraught with peril, Sarah's quick thinking and Evan's dogged determination had seen them through.

Evan studied Sarah's face, noticing her newfound resolve. Gone was the hesitance he'd detected early in their partnership, replaced by staunch conviction.

"I haven't always made it easy on you," Evan said ruefully. "When we started this quest, I didn't fully appreciate what we could accomplish together. But you've proven yourself an invaluable partner, Sarah. We complement each other perfectly."

Sarah tilted her head, amusement glinting in her eyes. "Getting philosophical on me, Dr. Reynolds? Don't tell me you're going soft."

Evan chuckled. "Maybe I am. Almost getting crushed by a collapsing tunnel has a way of putting things in perspective."

"Well, I like this new collaborative side of you," Sarah said. "But don't worry, I'll keep you on your toes. We're just getting started on unraveling this mystery."

Evan smiled, his earlier gloom dispelled. With Sarah's quick thinking and relentless curiosity, they would decipher the code and reveal its secrets. The past was not over with them yet.

Sarah's expression turned thoughtful as she traced her finger around the rim of her coffee cup. "When we started this, I saw you as an arrogant academic obsessed with his research. But you've shown real mettle on this journey. I guess we've both changed."

Evan nodded slowly, turning over her words. She was right—they'd both evolved during their shared quest.

"I used to think I could uncover the truth on my own through sheer determination," he admitted. "But I see now that real progress requires collaboration and different perspectives."

He met Sarah's gaze. "You've taught me the value of trusting others. My reluctance to accept help nearly got us both killed back in that booby-trapped tomb."

Sarah gave a wry smile. "You've shown me that risks are sometimes necessary to achieve real breakthroughs. I was too cautious at first, so focused on survival that I lost sight of the ultimate goal."

She raised her coffee in a toast. "To the lessons learned and obstacles overcome. May the next leg of our journey prove just as enlightening."

Evan clinked his cup against hers, camaraderie warming him more than the coffee. They still had challenges ahead, but together, they would conquer them. The truth was within their grasp.

Sarah took a sip of her coffee, contemplating their journey so far.

"My constant vigilance and distrust of others used to isolate me," she said pensively. "But with you, I've come to value companionship and real friendship."

She met Evan's eyes, her gaze new and vulnerable. "In watching your back, you've helped me open up. I see now that while caution is wise, connections with others make us stronger."

Evan nodded, touched by her honesty. "I never could have deciphered those ancient texts alone," he admitted. "Your different perspectives and areas of expertise were invaluable. Our friendship has taught me the power of collaboration."

He smiled warmly. "And I know I can always count on you to point out what I'm missing, keeping me grounded."

Sarah returned the smile. "We do make a good team," she agreed.

For a moment, they sat in comfortable silence; two explorers forged together through adversity. The bustling cafe around them faded, the noise dimming to a dull roar.

Finally, Evan raised his coffee mug. "To the adventures ahead," he said, eyes glinting with anticipation.

Sarah raised her mug. "And the strength we find in each other along the way."

Their mugs met with a resonant clink. The next leg of their journey awaited, but they would face it together.

Evan took a sip of his coffee, gathering his thoughts. "I need to thank you, Sarah," he began sincerely. "I never could have made it this far without you by my side."

Sarah looked surprised but pleased by his words. "What do you mean?" she asked.

"From the beginning, you've had my back," Evan explained. "When we were trapped in that cave, your ingenious idea led us to safety. And in the desert, I surely would have succumbed to the heat if not for your survival skills."

He shook his head in admiration. "Your quick thinking and resourcefulness have been invaluable at every turn. I don't know if I've ever properly expressed my gratitude."

Sarah smiled, touched. "It's meant a lot having you trust me," she replied. "Given my past, it wasn't easy for me to rely on someone else. But you've proven yourself an amazing partner - brilliant, determined, and caring."

She met his eyes earnestly. "I never could have deciphered those glyphs without your historical knowledge. And knowing you had my back gave me the courage to push past my limits."

Evan smiled back, moved by her words. For a moment, the bustling cafe faded away, and it was just the two of them - two explorers forged together by trust.

"Well, here's to many more adventures ahead," Evan said, raising his mug.

"Together," Sarah agreed, clinking her mug against his. They would face it as a team no matter what lay in store.

Sarah sipped her coffee, her mind drifting back over their journey.

"I can't believe some of our close calls," she mused. "Like that rickety rope bridge collapsing right after we crossed. Or the time we got cornered by those armed smugglers in the jungle."

Evan nodded gravely. "If not for your quick reflexes, we surely would've met our end. You kept a cool head under pressure."

"And you managed to talk us out of there," Sarah pointed out. "I don't know how you stayed so calm and rational."

"Well, we make a good team," Evan said. "Your street smarts and my book smarts complement each other nicely."

They shared a chuckle at that. Then Sarah grew pensive.

"I used to think I could tackle any challenge solo," she admitted. "But this journey has shown me how invaluable having someone you trust implicitly is."

Evan nodded in understanding. "And for me, it's been a lesson in opening up. I was so used to relying only on myself."

He met Sarah's eyes. "But I know now that true strength comes from partnerships built on loyalty."

Sarah smiled, moved by his words. "Well, here's to persevering together," she said, raising her mug again. "Whatever's around the next bend, we'll be ready."

Evan clinked his mug to hers, his eyes glinting with determination. The future was uncertain, but their bond was unshakable.

Evan and Sarah sat in comfortable silence for a few moments, sipping their drinks. The cafe's hustle and bustle faded into white noise as they enjoyed this rare moment of stillness.

Sarah gazed out the window, watching people rush by on the sidewalk. The morning light glinted off storefront windows and cast everything in a warm glow. Something was soothing about this little patch of calm amidst the kinetic energy of the city.

Evan studied the steam rising lazily from his coffee, lost in thought. His sharp mind oversaw the past few weeks' events, analyzing each discovery and plotting their next move. There were still missing pieces to this puzzle, but he felt they were getting close to a breakthrough.

Sarah turned back from the window to look at her friend. She knew Evan's pensive expression well. Evan's relentless curiosity drove them through all the setbacks and dead ends, and she admired that about him, even when his single-minded focus caused friction.

At this moment, though, his expression was content. The answers could wait a bit longer. It was enough to sit here with a friend, gathering strength for the road ahead.

Evan met Sarah's eyes and exchanged a knowing look. No words were needed. The future was uncertain, but they were ready for it—ready to unravel mysteries, face foes, and overcome obstacles—together.

After another minute of tranquil silence, Evan finished his coffee and set down the mug with a final touch.

"Shall we?" he said.

Sarah smiled and nodded. Their break was over adventure called.

Side by side, they stood up and headed for the door. The next chapter awaited them.

Chapter 17

The aroma of freshly brewed coffee permeated the quiet café as Evan and Sarah slid into the worn leather booth tucked away in the back corner. Shadows ringed their eyes, and a heaviness weighed upon their shoulders—the unmistakable mark of their recent ordeal.

As they settled in, their eyes met for a brief moment. A wealth of understanding passed between them in the span of a heartbeat. The sleepless nights puzzling over cryptic clues, the brushes with unsavory characters, the constant looking over their shoulders for unseen threats reflected at them in that shared gaze. No words were needed.

Evan ran a hand through his rumpled hair, his gaze drifting to the window as he gathered his thoughts. Sarah studied him from across the table, taking in the tension in his shoulders and the pinch between his brows. Her own body ached, her mind and spirit drained, but they'd made it through—together.

After a long moment, Evan turned back and offered her a tired smile. "I know I've said it before, but thank you again for sticking with me through all this madness. I couldn't have done it without you watching my back."

Sarah shook her head slightly, and pride and affection mingled with exhaustion in her voice. "You won't get rid of me that easily. We're in this together, partner."

They both knew the truth of her words. The journey had bound them, experiences woven together into an unbreakable thread. Whatever came next, they would face it side by side.

For now, the quiet café offered a moment's respite—a chance to breathe before the next adventure found them.

Sarah sighed long, leaning back in her chair as she regarded Evan thoughtfully. "I must admit, when you first told me about the scrolls, I thought you were chasing fairytales. But this..." She trailed off, shaking her head. "I never could have imagined where this path would lead us. The things we've seen..."

Evan nodded, a knowing look passing between them. They'd witnessed wonders beyond imagination and unearthed secrets lost to time. But it had come at a cost—sleepless nights, injuries, and a brush with dangers, both human and otherwise.

"When we started, I don't think either of us expected how high the stakes would become," he said. "But you never faltered, not for a second."

Sarah gave a wry half-smile. "Oh, I faltered. But one look at you, so determined to follow the trail wherever it led, I knew I couldn't let you go on alone."

She reached across the table, briefly squeezing his hand. The simple contact carried a wealth of meaning: gratitude, respect, and the bond forged between them. They would take it together no matter where the next step of their journey led.

After a moment, Sarah withdrew her hand and glanced around the cafe. It was a temporary oasis of calm, but she knew they couldn't stay long. There was still much work to be done, secrets left to uncover. The thrill of the chase called to them both.

"Well, partner," she said, meeting Evan's gaze. "Are you Ready for whatever comes next?"

Sarah's eyes took on a faraway look as she contemplated Evan's words. This journey had irrevocably changed them both. The long days, sleepless nights, brushes of danger, and euphoria of discovery had all left their mark.

"I never imagined how this would change me," she said quietly. "When we started, I thought it was just another expedition. But it's become so much more."

She absently traced her fingers over faint scars on her hands - reminders of traps evaded, obstacles overcome.

"I used to think I had everything figured out—my work, my life, who I was." She ruefully shook her head. "But out there, hunting for clues, none of that mattered. It was like I'd been broken open and put back together differently."

Sarah lifted her gaze to Evan's, resolving to harden her eyes.

"I know there's no going back to the way things were, and I'm glad for that. I feel...stronger now. More focused. The things we've seen, what we're trying to protect—I'll do whatever it takes." Her voice rang with conviction.

She reached for Evan's hand again, gripping it tightly. "Whatever comes next, we're in it together. Always."

Their bond had been forged through fire and steel. They'd emerged indelibly marked by the crucible of their shared quest. Wherever the road led, they would walk it side by side.

Evan nodded slowly, a thoughtful look crossing his face.

"You're right," he said. "This hasn't just been about the treasure. It's changed us - opened our eyes in ways we never expected."

He leaned back in his chair, gazing out the cafe window. "We've seen incredible things. I learned so much about cultures and histories most will never know. But it came with a cost."

His eyes darkened briefly before he turned back to Sarah. "We took huge risks. And we'll carry those scars forever, inside and out."

Evan clasped her hand warmly. "But you know what? I'd do it all again in a heartbeat. Because the rewards were so much greater than gold or jewels."

He paused, searching for the right words. "It's like we uncovered a new world of knowledge and meaning. Things that can't be quantified or displayed in a museum. Those are the real treasures."

Sarah's eyes lit up with understanding.

"You're right," she said softly. "The journey itself was the greatest gift. Everything we experienced together - that's something no one can ever take away."

She smiled then, some of the shadow lifting from her face. The future was uncertain, but they would face it arm in arm, bound by all they'd seen and done. Their lives were forever changed, and they wouldn't have it any other way.

Sarah nodded slowly, contemplating Evan's words.

"You're right," she said. "This quest has impacted us profoundly in ways we're still processing."

She leaned forward, her voice lowering. "Professionally, it's been a game-changer. The knowledge we've gained about those ancient cultures is priceless - it will transform our work."

Evan's eyes lit up. "Just imagine the research papers we could publish, the insights we could share with the academic community."

"Exactly," said Sarah. "We are now responsible for documenting our findings and adding to the historical record. Our adventure mustn't be for nothing."

Evan gripped her hand excitedly. "And think what this means for preservation efforts. We must protect these ancient sites and artifacts."

His tone grew serious. "After seeing that forgotten temple firsthand, I'm more committed than ever to safeguarding humanity's heritage."

Sarah nodded, resolve in her eyes. "We can't let greed or exploitation destroy these links to our collective past. Too much has already been lost."

She sat back, gazing into the distance as if visualizing the work ahead. "If our experience has taught us anything, the past still has so much to teach us. We have to keep those pathways open."

Evan smiled at his colleague, this kindred spirit who had stood by him. "Then that's our mission - ensuring those treasures survive for future generations. That the journey continues..."

Sarah gazed out the café window, the weight of their recent trials etched on her face. Though she tried to hide it, Evan could see the toll their perilous quest had taken.

"I won't lie; this has been the greatest challenge of my career," she said finally, turning back to meet his eyes. "The riddles, the traps, the enemies at every turn...I've never felt so tested."

Evan nodded, swirling the dregs of coffee in his cup. "Or so unsure we'd make it out alive," he added grimly.

Sarah managed a weak smile. "If not for you watching my back, I might not have." She reached across the table to squeeze his hand. "I can never thank you enough, Evan."

"Hey, we looked out for each other," he said. "I couldn't have cracked those glyphs without you."

"Still, knowing you were there gave me strength to keep going when all seemed lost." Sarah blinked back tears, revealing the depth of her anguish. "This quest came at a cost, no denying it."

Evan felt his composure falter. "You're right. We've been changed by this, Sarah." His voice grew thick with emotion. "But we saw it through together. That's what matters."

Sarah met his gaze, relief flooding her face. Whatever they had endured, at least they had come through it side by side. At that moment, Evan knew their bond was unbreakable. The past could not defeat them, not as long as they stood united.

Sarah took a deep breath, composing herself. "I know I said I regretted coming on this quest with you. But the truth is, I wouldn't trade it for anything." She gave him a tender smile. "You brought out the best in me, Evan. It made me find courage and resilience I didn't know I had."

Evan felt his chest swell with affection. "I was just thinking the same about you," he admitted. "I couldn't have completed this without your quick thinking and determination." He shook his head in amazement. "You're the bravest person. I know, Sarah."

She chuckled softly. "Only because you inspire me to be brave." Her expression grew thoughtful. "I used to be so cynical, you know? Suspicious of everyone's motives." She glanced down. "But you taught me to have faith again - in myself, in people."

Evan nodded, moved by her words. "Well, I've gained a new appreciation for life from you. Almost losing it makes you see what matters." He smiled gently. "Like the chance to share adventures with someone you..." He trailed off, suddenly shy.

Sarah's eyes lit up, reading his meaning. "I feel the same way," she said softly. "This quest brought us closer than I imagined possible." She squeezed his hand. "Whatever the future holds, I'm glad we'll face it together."

Evan smiled back, his heart full. The treasure they'd found was so much more precious than gold or jewels. It was a bond forged by fire, emerging more vital than ever. With Sarah by his side, he was ready for whatever came next.

Sarah glanced at her watch and sighed. "I suppose we should get going. Our work is far from over."

Evan nodded reluctantly. There would be more mysteries to unravel and more questions to answer. But they now had the tools and knowledge to pursue them.

He stood, extending his hand to help Sarah up. She grasped it firmly, smiling at his eyes. In that shared look, there was a world of understanding. The future was uncertain, but they would tackle it as a team.

Stepping outside, they both took a deep breath of the cool night air. The sky was clear, the stars twinkling with promise. The café's lights cast a warm glow behind them as they walked away, side by side. The adventure continued, but they were no longer the same people who had started it. More vital, wiser, bonded by tribulation, they moved forward purposefully. The true treasure was within them all along.

Chapter 18

Evan's flashlight cut through the darkness, illuminating the vast underground chamber. Sarah gasped as the light revealed piles of glittering artifacts and ancient relics, untouched for centuries. Her heart pounded with exhilaration and apprehension.

"We made it," Evan whispered. His voice echoed off the cavern walls.

Sarah's eyes darted around the room. Intricate carvings and hieroglyphs adorned the stone surfaces, their meanings still mysterious. She paused at an onyx statue of Anubis, its eyes seeming to follow her.

What secrets do you hold? She wondered.

Evan lowered his flashlight, shadows dancing across his rugged face. "This is everything we've been searching for."

Sarah nodded slowly, the gravity of their discovery sinking in. After years of deciphering obscure texts and evading those who wanted to exploit this knowledge, they had finally arrived.

Evan rubbed his forehead, feeling the toll of their recent struggles. But it had all been worth it. Glancing at Sarah, he knew she felt the same weariness and hope.

Sarah moved further into the chamber, running her fingers along the hieroglyphs. Each symbol unlocked a piece of the puzzle. But there were still missing fragments.

"We're close," she said. "The final clues must be here somewhere."

Evan joined her, reinvigorated by her determination. Together, they would unravel the secrets of this ancient place and ensure its wonders were preserved for all humanity. This was the moment they had been waiting for.

Sarah's eyes suddenly narrowed as she noticed Evan wince slightly.

"You're hurt," she said, moving towards him with concern.

Evan shook his head dismissively. "It's nothing."

But Sarah could see the gash on his arm, a lingering reminder of their arduous journey here. She rifled through her backpack and pulled out a first aid kit.

"Here, let me take a look."

Evan reluctantly relented as Sarah examined the wound, her brows furrowed in concentration. She cleaned and dressed it with gentle but deft hands, applying an antibiotic ointment. Evan watched her, once again struck by her compassion and competence.

"That should hold for now," Sarah said, meeting his gaze. In that shared look was an unspoken bond forged through their trials. Evan saw their mission's toll on Sarah, too, from the new lines on her face to the wariness in her eyes. But her spirit remained unbroken.

"Thank you," he said softly.

Sarah smiled and nodded, understanding the depths of those two simple words. They had sacrificed much to be here, both willing to risk everything for this discovery. But they had each other. And together, they would see this through to the end.

Sarah secured the bandage around Evan's arm and gently rolled his sleeve back down. He nodded in gratitude, then turned his focus back to the ancient chamber.

They were surrounded by intricate carvings and symbols, clues to unlocking the secret they sought. Evan's eyes darted around, taking it all in. Sarah did the same, mentally cataloging each engraving and artifact.

"Look there," Evan said, pointing to a relief depicting a series of celestial markers - the key to deciphering the codex in his bag.

Sarah's gaze followed his outstretched hand. "You're right; that must be the Rosetta stone we need."

He stepped closer, brow furrowed in concentration as she studied the images. Evan joined her, excitement rising in his chest. They were so close now.

Suddenly, Sarah tensed. Her eyes locked on a barely perceptible indentation along the chamber wall. Reaching out, she pressed it firmly. The stone depressed with a grinding click.

Evan's eyes widened. "Sarah, what did you..."

Before he could finish, the wall began to shift. Stone scraped against stone as a hidden doorway swung slowly open. The passage it revealed disappeared into inky darkness.

Evan turned to Sarah, shock giving way to awe. She met his gaze, triumph flickering across her face.

"Shall we?"

Evan and Sarah stepped into the passage without hesitation, the darkness swallowing them. Sarah clicked on her flashlight, the narrow beam cutting through the blackness. The passage sloped steadily downward, the air growing colder.

Evan ran his hand along the rough stone walls as they descended. In the flashlight's glow, strange markings and half-eroded carvings emerged.

"This must lead to the inner sanctum," he murmured. "All the secrets are down there."

Sarah nodded. "Let's hope we can find them before the Order does."

They pressed on, the passage twisting and turning. Evan visualized the layout in his mind's eye, tracing their path. After fifteen minutes, he guessed they were at least a hundred feet beneath the surface.

Suddenly, the passage opened into a massive chamber. Sarah swung her flashlight in an arc, illuminating towering stone pillars that disappeared into the gloom above. The scale was breathtaking.

Evan's voice echoed as he spoke. "Incredible...this place could've been lost for centuries."

Sarah paused, shining her light on the chamber floor. Strange symbols surrounded the central dais. "Look there, that must be it."

Evan followed her gaze. His pulse quickened. After everything, the secrets of the ancients were finally within reach.

Sarah swept her flashlight over the central dais, illuminating an intricately carved pedestal. Atop it was a small artifact—an obsidian cube covered in alien hieroglyphs and abstract symbols. Evan's eyes widened. This had to be the key to deciphering the ancient knowledge hidden within these ruins.

He joined Sarah at the base of the dais, craning his neck to examine the artifact. It seemed to draw him in, pulsing with an otherworldly energy.

"This is it," he breathed. "The heart of the mystery."

Sarah nodded, her expression is solemn. "I can feel its power. This is what the Order was searching for."

Reverently, Evan reached out and lifted the cube from its pedestal. He expected it to be ice cold, but it was warm, vibrating in his palms. The symbols flashed in an incomprehensible code.

Sarah also touched it, gasping as the energy jolted through her. The flashlight fell from her grip, plunging them into darkness. Only the artifact gave a faint glow, bathing them in an eerie bluish light.

"What do you think it does?" Sarah whispered. The shadows made her face look skeletal.

Evan turned the cube over in his hands. "I'm not sure, but we're meant to unlock its secrets," he said.

He ran his fingers over the cryptic hieroglyphs. There had to be a pattern, a codex, something...

Suddenly, the markings began to shift, the cube growing warmer. Ancient knowledge unlocked...a gateway opening...

Evan and Sarah exchanged stunned looks as the cube began to glow brighter, the strange symbols swirling across its surfaces. It hovered above their palms, no longer needing to be held.

"What's happening?" Sarah breathed.

Before Evan could respond, a beam of light shot out from the artifact, illuminating the chamber. The light coalesced into a shimmering hologram depicting an ancient Egyptian landscape. Glyphs and symbols floated through the air as a booming voice spoke in a language they could not comprehend.

"It's a projection, a message!" Evan realized. He studied the images flashing before them, piecing together the meaning. "This is incredible - it contains the accumulated knowledge of their civilization!"

Sarah's eyes shone with awe as she took in the spectacle. "More than just knowledge. This is their history, their wisdom..."

The booming voice quieted, and the projection zoomed in on a group of robed figures gathered around a fire. One of them turned, seeming to make eye contact with Evan and Sarah across the centuries.

Evan shivered. "He sees us," he murmured. "They meant for us to find this, to learn their secrets."

"It's a gift," Sarah said softly. "A guide they left for future generations. This treasure was never just about gold or jewels..."

Evan nodded. "It's a map - a way to unlock humanity's potential." He took Sarah's hand, both still reeling with the revelation. "Our journey brought us here for a reason."

The projection faded, and the cube went dark. Evan and Sarah stood in awe, and this discovery forever changed their destiny. The true treasure had been within their grasp all along.

Evan and Sarah retraced their steps through the twisting underground labyrinth with renewed purpose. The cold stone walls seemed to radiate an energy now, ancient symbols flickering in the dim light.

"All this time, it was leading us here," Evan said, hand trailing along the wall. "We just had to learn how to read the signs."

Sarah nodded, her archaeologist's eye tracing each glyph and carving. "It makes me wonder what other secrets are still hidden, waiting to be found."

They turned a corner, and Evan winced, hand going to his bandaged arm. Sarah steadied him.

"Once we're out, I'll get that properly treated," she said, her eyes filled with concern.

Evan gave a pained smile. "I've endured worse for less reward." His gaze held meaning.

Sarah flushed, glancing away. Their bond had grown on this journey, an unspoken understanding passing whenever their eyes met.

After long moments navigating the maze, they arrived back at the treasure chamber. Sarah helped Evan over the threshold, the sight of the gold and jewels now secondary to the more excellent knowledge they had uncovered.

"We'll keep it safe," Evan said, resting a hand on an engraved pillar. "They meant for us to inherit their legacy."

Sarah placed a hand on his shoulder, meeting his unwavering gaze. "And we will honor that responsibility."

Together, they turned to leave, the future shining as bright as the treasure behind them. The true riches were not material but what they now carried in their hearts.

Sarah entered the sunlight, squinting against the brightness after the dim passageways below. She took a deep breath, revitalized by the fresh air after the dank underground air.

Beside her, Evan blinked rapidly, eyes adjusting. He gazed at the vista before them - endless dunes and a fierce blue sky.

"I'll never take this for granted again," he said. Sarah knew he didn't just mean the sunlight.

"Me neither." She turned to him. "The next part won't be easy, with the Order after us. But we've got this." She held up the artifact in the demonstration.

Evan's eyes crinkled with his smile. "Together, we can do anything." He lifted his hand, and Sarah clasped it without hesitation. The trials had forged an unbreakable bond between them.

They stood a moment longer, soaking in the landscape that seemed to stretch forever. The rolling dunes held their secrets, mysteries waiting to be unearthed.

Sarah tugged at Evan's hand. "Come on. Let's go chart the next adventure."

His grin widened, and he let her lead the way, the promise of discovery shining in both their eyes. The artifact was only the first step. Their true journey was beginning.

Sarah took the first step down the dune, her boots sinking into the soft sand. The exertion made her injured leg ache, but she gritted her teeth against the pain. There would be time to rest later. They needed to distance themselves from this place before the Order tracked them down.

Evan followed close behind, one hand pressed to his bandaged ribs. Sarah glanced back at him with concern. "How's the wound?"

"I'll live," he said wryly.

Sarah huffed a laugh. Please leave it to Evan to make light of a near-death experience. Her smile faded as she recalled how close it had been this time. If she hadn't reached him when she did...

She banished the thought. He was here beside her; that's what mattered.

The terrain grew steeper as they descended, their pace slowing. Sarah's eyes continuously scanned their surroundings, watchful for any sign of pursuit. She wouldn't put it past the Order to have tracked them by now.

Evan seemed to read her thoughts. "We should find shelter before nightfall. Somewhere defensible."

Sarah nodded. The artifact felt heavy in her pack. So many had died for its secrets, and they could not let it fall back into the Order's hands.

Sarah spotted a rocky outcropping ahead as the sun sank lower on the horizon. It would provide cover and a vantage point.

"There," she said, angling towards the promise of rest at the end of this long day's journey.

And tomorrow, a new adventure will begin...

Chapter 19

The sun was setting over the ancient city of Thebes, casting an orange glow over the towering ruins. Dr. Evan Reynolds stood at the edge of the temple complex, staring out at the horizon. He had finally done it - uncovered the long-lost tomb of Ramses III.

"Congratulations, Evan," Sarah said, coming up behind him. "This is incredible."

"Thanks, Sarah," Evan replied, smiling. "I couldn't have done it without you."

As they turned to leave, they heard footsteps approaching. Anton and Nadia stepped out behind a pillar, flanked by several armed men.

"Hello, Dr. Reynolds," Anton said, a smirk on his face. "I believe congratulations are in order."

"Anton," Evan said, his voice cold. "What are you doing here?"

"Taking what's rightfully mine," Anton replied, gesturing towards the tomb.

"Over my dead body," Evan said, stepping forward.

"Careful now, Doctor," Anton said. "I wouldn't want anything to happen to you or your lovely colleague here."

Evan glanced over at Sarah, who had her hand on the hilt of her knife. They both knew they were outnumbered and outgunned.

"Fine," Evan said, holding up his hands. "Take it. But know that history will remember you as nothing but a thief."

"The victors write history," Anton said, grinning. "And I always win."

With that, Anton and his men entered the tomb, leaving Evan and Sarah standing outside.

"Damn it," Sarah muttered under her breath.

"Let them have their victory," Evan said, touching her shoulder. "We'll get them next time."

"Next time?" Sarah asked, raising an eyebrow.

"Next time," Evan repeated a glint in his eye. "Because we're not done yet."

As they walked away, Evan couldn't help but feel a sense of excitement. They had uncovered something incredible, and he knew more secrets were waiting to be unlocked. He just had to figure out how to beat Anton at his game.

Epilogue

Three months had passed since the dust settled on the streets of Cairo, the echoes of their final confrontation fading into the annals of their extraordinary adventure. Dr. Alexander Kane sat in his study, surrounded by piles of his notes and the remnants of the Osiris Code, now safely locked away where no greedy hands could reach. The sunset outside his window cast long shadows across the room that seemed to whisper secrets still hidden in the world's dark corners.

Elena Ramirez leaned against the doorway, watching Alex with a smile that spoke of shared secrets and hard-won trust. They had survived the unimaginable, their lives intertwined by danger and desire, and now they were partners in more than just their quest. Their relationship, forged in the fires of adversity, had blossomed into a deep, abiding love that promised to withstand the tests of time.

Detective Mike Thompson, now back in the United States, had been instrumental in dismantling Viktor Petrov's network. With Petrov behind bars and his criminal empire in ruins, Thompson was finally able to close the case that had consumed his life for months. His career had taken a turn for the better, with commendations and respect from his peers, yet his thoughts often drifted back to his time in Egypt, to the people who had changed the course of his investigation and his life.

In a quiet cafe in Rome, Isabella Cruz sat alone, sipping her coffee and watching the bustling street. Her alliance with Petrov had been opportunistic, and her betrayal was calculated to secure her escape. Now, she could start over with a new identity and a small fortune. Yet, freedom came with its costs, and she longed for a redemption she wasn't sure she deserved.

Alex turned from his desk to meet Elena's gaze in the study. "It’s over isn't it?" he asked, though he already knew the answer.

"It's over for now," Elena replied, wrapping her arms around him. "But who knows what the future holds, Alex? With you, I'm ready for anything."

As they stood together, the world outside continued its relentless pace, oblivious to the ancient secrets they had protected and the future they had secured. The treasures of the Osiris Code were no longer a threat but a promise of mysteries yet to come. As the night drew its veil over the day, Alexander Kane and Elena Ramirez faced the future as guardians of the past, their love a beacon in a world that thrived on shadows and light.

Thus, the story of the Osiris Code closed, but the doors to new adventures were beginning to open.

We Value Your Feedback!

Dear Reader,

Thank you for choosing this book and embarking on this journey with us. We hope that you found the content enlightening and engaging. Your opinion is precious to us and potential readers trying to decide whether this book is right for them.

If you enjoyed your experience, please leave a review. Your insights and feedback help us improve and assist other readers in making informed choices. Whether it's a few words of encouragement or detailed thoughts on what resonated with you, every review makes a difference.

Sharing your review is easy:

Where to Leave a Review: You can post your thoughts on the platform where you purchased the book or any book review website you frequent.

What to Include: Feel free to share what you loved, what surprised you, or even what you think could be improved. Your honest opinion is what we're after!

Reviews are an excellent way to communicate with us and a great opportunity to help shape the community and discussions around this book.

Thank you once again for your support and trust. We can't wait to read your thoughts!

Warm regards,
Marcus Flint

Milton Keynes UK
Ingram Content Group UK Ltd.
UKHW021029270524
443319UK00017B/1022